THE MAGIC FARAWAY TREE

~ A NEW ~
ADVENTURE

Look out for these other Faraway Tree stories by

Enid Blyton

The Enchanted Wood
The Magic Faraway Tree
The Folk of the Faraway Tree
Adventure of the Goblin Dog

Picture books:
The Magic Faraway Tree: Silky's Story
The Magic Faraway Tree: Moonface's Story

THE MAGIC FARAWAY TREE

Illustrated by
MARK BEECH

~A NEW ADVENTURE

Inspired by
Enid Blyton

JACQUELINE WILSON

Hodder
Children's
Books

HODDER CHILDREN'S BOOKS
First published in Great Britain in 2022 by Hodder & Stoughton Limited

5 7 9 10 8 6 4

A CIP catalogue record for this book is available from the British Library.

Hardback: 978 1 444 96337 3
Waterstones edition: 978 1 444 96888 0

Paperback: 978 1 444 96338 0
Trade paperback: 978 1 444 96341 0

Typeset in Caslon Twelve by Avon DataSet Ltd, Alcester, Warwickshire

Printed and bound in Great Britain by Clays Ltd, Elcograf S.p.A.

The paper and board used in this book are
made from wood from responsible sources.

Hodder Children's Books
An imprint of Hachette Children's Group
Part of Hodder & Stoughton Limited
Carmelite House
50 Victoria Embankment
London EC4Y 0DZ

An Hachette UK Company
www.hachette.co.uk
www.hachettechildrens.co.uk

For Alexandra Antscherl
With love

CHAPTER ONE

MUM AND Dad got in the front of the car, and the three children climbed in the back. It was quite a squash, because Birdy insisted on taking her dog, Gilbert, too. He wasn't a real dog. Mum had won him at a fair. His fur was bright turquoise and his eyes were crossed and everyone else thought he was hideous, but Birdy loved him passionately. He was almost as big as she was, so she couldn't balance him comfortably on her lap. He wouldn't fit on the floor, so Milo and Mia were forced to let him have a share of the back seat, though they moaned about it. Forcefully.

'Pipe down, you lot. We're on holiday! No squabbling!' said Dad.

Milo and Mia exchanged glances. Birdy was definitely Dad's favourite, just because she was the youngest and acted cute, often deliberately. Her real name was Bethany, but they all called her Birdy because when she was a baby she used to make a funny cheep-cheep sound before revving up into a full-blooded wail.

Milo was the eldest and the only boy. He liked playing video games and making things with wood and most of all he loved running. He wasn't that great at most sporty things, but he was brilliant at running. He'd just won the school cup for best runner on Sports Day, though some of the children were a lot older than him.

His teacher had suggested he train properly down at the sports centre this summer. Milo wanted to do this very badly, but they were going to stay at this cottage in the country for the entire summer. He wanted to go on holiday, but he wished he could have done this special running course too. Even if it meant not *going* on holiday. He loved his family, but he didn't always like being cooped up with them all the time.

He stared out of the window and imagined running along beside the car and then veering off over a meadow, on and on, over a distant hill, and up above the clouds into the great blue sky.

Milo's daydream was so real he was actually puffing gently.

'Milo! Stop breathing all over me!' Mia said. She was in the middle, between her bony brother and hairy Gilbert, and could hardly manage to draw breath herself. Even though her elbows were pinned to her sides she was trying to draw in her sketchbook. She drew real dogs, magnificent German shepherds and beautiful huskies, and the pigs and cows and sheep she was looking forward to seeing in the countryside. By the time she'd branched off into exotic wild animals, tigers and elephants and bears, she was starting to feel sick. Very, very sick.

Dad had to stop the car where Mia *was* very, very sick, and annoyingly she still felt queasy when they stopped at a motorway service station. Mum and Dad had fish and chips, Milo and Birdy had McDonald's, and Mia had two spoonfuls of tomato soup and then had to go outside with Mum. She didn't mind too much, because a man had tied up his Labrador while he popped inside for a takeaway and Mia made friends with him. The Labrador was first attracted by the plate of chips Mum had taken with her, but soon fell in love with Mia and nuzzled into her adoringly.

'Oh, Mum, if *only* I could have a dog,' she said, for the millionth time.

'I know,' said Mum. 'Still, we've got Gilbert.'

She was trying to joke. Mia gave her a look.

They lived on a small estate where you weren't allowed to have dogs. Or even cats. Mum and Dad said she could have a budgie or a hamster indoors, but Mia didn't feel it was fair to keep a bird or an animal in a cage.

The man came back and took his Labrador away. Mia sighed. She was still feeling a bit wobbly. She leant against Mum.

'When I grow up I'm going to be a vet,' she said. 'Then I'll be with animals all day long.'

'That's a very good idea,' said Mum.

They were standing beside an ice-cream stall.

'Do you know what?' said Mia. 'I think an ice cream might make me feel a bit better.'

Dad and Milo and Birdy came out of the café

when Mia was halfway through her Whippy.

'That's not fair!' they said.

So they all had ice creams and then got back in the car. They had the windows wide open this time and Mum wouldn't let Mia draw in case she made herself sick again. Mia got a bit bored.

'When I grow up I'm going to be a vet,' she told the rest of the family. 'And I'll make every single one of my animal patients better. I might even get to be a vet on television because I'll be so good at it.'

'No you won't,' said Milo. 'You have to be ever so brainy to be a vet, and you're hopeless at maths.'

Milo was secretly worried that Mia was cleverer than him. He was always relieved when she couldn't do sums.

'I might get better at it,' said Mia. 'What do you want to be when you're grown-up then?'

'Easy-peasy,' said Milo. 'I'm going to be an athlete. An Olympic standard runner!'

'Go, Milo!' said Dad, laughing. 'And what about you, Birdy? What do you want to be when you grow up, sweetheart?'

Birdy considered this carefully while she stroked Gilbert's matted fur. Then her face lit up.

'I'm going to be a fairy!' she said.

'Yuck!' said Milo.

'Oh, Birdy! You don't still believe in fairies, do you?' said Mia.

'Yes, I do,' said Birdy firmly. She loved fairies. She had a fairy costume, with a pink satin top and a sticky-out net skirt, and if she had her way she'd wear it all the time, even to school. She also had a magic wand, though it refused to turn Milo and Mia into toads. She had a shelf of fairy books too. She wasn't very good at reading yet, but she'd heard them so often she could simply look at the lovely pictures and mutter the stories to herself. Deep down she knew it wasn't very probable that she could become a real fairy, but she liked pretending.

'I don't see why Birdy can't be a fairy,' said Dad. 'It's a lovely idea. Maybe I'll be a fairy when I'm grown-up!'

This made them all laugh. Then they sang songs in the car and played I spy, though Birdy's clues were unreliable. But after a while they grew tired and fidgety.

'Aren't we nearly there *yet*?' they kept asking.

'Soon,' said Mum, but soon never came.

The satnav on their car didn't seem to be working properly. Mum fished in the glove compartment for an old atlas and peered at what she thought was the right page.

'It's weird, we should be here!' she said, stabbing at a patch of green. 'Hey, guess what this foresty bit is called. The Enchanted Wood!'

'Seriously?' said Milo.

'Enchanted, like in a fairy tale?' asked Mia.

'The Enchanted Wood!' Birdy whispered and shivered with excitement.

They all peered out of the car windows for this strangely named wood.

'Any sign of it?' said Dad.

'Not so much as a branch,' said Mum, looking left.

But the three children suddenly shouted, '*There it is!*'

It was on the right, still quite far away, a large

dark-green wood, the trees very thick and tall and close together. One tree seemed to grow up and up and up, so high that the top was covered in cloud, though the rest of the sky was clear blue.

Dad carried on driving down the main road until he came to a right turning with a very old signpost. They had to squint to make out the words. TO THE ENCHANTED WOOD. And someone had chalked a word underneath, and underlined it. CAUTION!

'What does that mean?' Birdy asked.

'It means be careful. Maybe you can get easily lost in the woods,' said Mum.

'Maybe there are ghoulies and goblins there,' Milo joked, pulling a face and turning his hands into claws.

'Maybe there are wolves still breeding there,' Mia said, only half joking.

'Maybe there are fairies,' breathed Birdy. She wasn't joking at all. She was hoping like anything she was right.

'Maybe *you* can be the fairy in your little pink dress,' said Dad, as the car bumped along the narrowing lane. 'Hey, I wonder if the "caution" bit is to tell you this lane isn't suitable for vehicles!'

The lane kept twisting and turning, until they lost all sense of direction.

'I'm starting to feel sick again,' Mia warned.

'I think it must be a dead end,' said Mum. 'Hadn't we better turn round?'

'No, wait! There's a cottage up ahead!' said Dad.

'The advert said it was called Rose Cottage,' said Mum.

'Well, look – there are the roses!' said Dad, pulling the car to a stop in front of a wonderful little picture-book cottage. It had white-washed walls and a thatched roof and a red door with yellow honeysuckle growing in an arch around it. There was a crimson rose bush either side of the door, and more roses rioting in the garden – red and pink and white and apricot and yellow and even pale purple.

The children tumbled out of the car, Birdy dragging Gilbert, breathing in the heady scent of the roses.

'Wow!' said Milo.

A NEW ADVENTURE

'I love it here!' said Mia.

'It's magic!' said Birdy.

Mum found the key box at the side of the cottage and typed in the numbers shown on the letter she'd received. It opened up and she took out the key. It shone brightly in the afternoon sunlight.

'It's gold!' said Birdy. 'Perhaps it's a magic key and this is a magic cottage!'

'And there are little pixie people living inside,' said Milo, mocking her gently.

'And little bunnies who can talk and little squirrels in aprons who do all the housework,' said Mia, joining in.

Birdy's lip quivered, realising they were teasing her.

'Don't be mean to my Birdy!' said Dad, picking her up. 'I think it *is* a magic cottage. It's *our* magic cottage for the whole summer and we're going to have a magic holiday.'

Mum opened the red door with the gold key.

'We'll go in first, Your Ladyship,' Dad said to Birdy, and carried her inside. The door was small and Dad was tall, so he bumped his head, but he laughed it off. Mum and Milo and Mia followed.

They stepped straight into the living room. It had a soft green sofa and three small, comfy chairs – one red, one blue and one pink. Milo's favourite colour just happened to be red, Mia's blue and Birdy's pink. It really did seem like magic, though there were no bunnies saying hello and not a single squirrel dusting the ornaments.

There was a small kitchen with a stove and a scrubbed table and a larder, some windy stairs, and two bedrooms and a bathroom on the next floor. The first bedroom was small, but it had a big bed with a green and red and blue and pink patchwork quilt.

'That's Mum and Dad's room, and we can all get in their bed for a cuddle in the morning,' said Birdy.

The second room was smaller still, but it had two single beds with quilts all different colours of the rainbow.

'Birdy and I will share, like we do at home,' said Mia.

'But where am I going to sleep?' Milo asked.

'In the bath!' said Mia, laughing.

'There must be another attic room upstairs,' said Mum, pointing to a tiny flight of stairs not much bigger than a ladder.

They all went up the stairs to look, though Mum had to bend her head and Dad had to crouch right down. It was an amazing little room with a round window in the thatch. There was only space for a small bed with another rainbow quilt and a tiny cupboard and a round rag rug on the wooden floorboards. Milo and Mia and Birdy all wanted it to be their room.

'Tell you what, why don't you take it in turns? Each of you have the room for one week. Then you'll all have another turn before we go home, as we're here for six weeks,' said Mum.

'And I'll go first because I'm the oldest!' said Milo.

'That's not fair!' said Mia, who was secretly counting on her fingers, working it out.

'Can I still have my six turns?' said Birdy, who hadn't started learning sums yet.

They had a lucky dip to decide who'd have the

bedroom first when they were eating their tea. They had baked potatoes with cheese and a tomato salad and then a little pot of strawberry yoghurt each with a chocolate toffee from a tin for a treat.

'Whoever chooses the purple toffee gets to sleep in the attic bedroom first,' said Mum. 'You three shut your eyes tight.'

Dad put his big hands over their eyes so they couldn't possibly cheat. Though he might have opened his fingers just a chink when it was Birdy's turn to pick a toffee. She got the purple one! But Milo and Mia didn't mind too much because they were allowed two toffees each as consolation prizes.

They went for a walk after tea to stretch their legs. The three children all wanted to go to the Enchanted Wood, but it had turned cloudy now and Mum and Dad decided it was too dark to explore it properly. They walked down the lane all the way to the nearest village. There was a pub with fairy lights in the garden so they sat there instead. The children all had cola and crisps even though they'd recently had tea.

'It's the start of our holiday after all,' said Mum, clinking glasses with Dad.

Then they walked all the way home. Dad had to give Birdy a piggyback. The children begged to stay up late when they got back to the cottage, but they were all rubbing their eyes and yawning. Mum and Dad came up together to kiss Milo and Mia goodnight in their twin beds. Then they struggled up the tiny stairs to tuck Birdy up in her little bed.

'Are you sure you're going to be all right up here by yourself, poppet?' Mum asked.

'Yes, I absolutely love it!' said Birdy.

'You're like a real little bird up here in your nest,' said Dad. He gave her his torch in case she needed to come down the stairs in the night, and Mum tucked her up under the covers, Gilbert stuffed in beside her.

Birdy waited until they were safely downstairs, and then she untucked herself to peer out of the window. She wanted to look out at the Enchanted Wood, but it was too dark to see it now. She tried shining the torch at the window, but the light bounced back into her room, not showing her anything. She switched the torch off – but still saw a little glimmering in the dark. It got nearer. Nearer and nearer. Right up to the window. Birdy saw beautiful golden hair, a sparkly dress and a pair of shining silvery wings.

'A fairy!' Birdy whispered in awe.

CHAPTER TWO

BIRDY PUT her hand to the glass and the fairy put out her hand too, her fingers splayed in exactly the same shape. Birdy felt a strange tingle right up her arm. She was almost holding hands with a fairy! She didn't look like any of the fairies in her books or any of the Disney films, but she knew the golden being the other side of the glass was quite definitely a fairy with real wings. She wasn't small like a butterfly, she was as big as Birdy herself which made it even more exciting.

She mouthed, '*Hello!*' at the fairy, and the fairy mouthed it back to her, and then smiled. Birdy

wondered if she could manage the latch on her window to let the fairy into her bedroom, but it was too stiff to budge. The fairy gave a little shrug and then mouthed something else. Birdy couldn't quite make it out. The fairy patiently tried again.

'*Come to my house tomorrow!*'

'Where?' Birdy said out loud.

The fairy said something else. Birdy tried hard to understand. *The Faraway Sea?*

'Can you say it again?' she begged.

'Birdy?' Mum was standing at the bottom of the stairs!

'Mum, come here!' Birdy called.

The fairy shook her head quickly, blew Birdy a kiss and then flew away.

'Oh, come back, please!' said Birdy, but the fairy was already far away herself, just a tiny glimmer in the darkness.

'I'm here, darling,' said Mum, running into the room. 'What are you doing by the window?'

'I was talking to a fairy. I wanted you to see her,' said Birdy.

'Oh, Birdy!' Mum gave her a hug. 'You're having a dream, darling. Come on, back to bed.'

'No, I don't want to!' said Birdy, trying to wriggle away from Mum.

'Oh, dear, is it a bit too lonely up here? You can come in with Dad and me if you like,' said Mum.

'No, I love it here. I want to see the fairy again,' Birdy explained.

'You and your fairies,' said Mum. 'Well, hop back into this bed then, and I'll stay with you for a little bit till you calm down.'

'Can't I wait by the window?' Birdy asked.

'No, you absolutely cannot! You'll be trying to climb out next,' said Mum worriedly. She tried the window latch herself, but couldn't budge it either. 'Thank goodness!' she said. 'You might be our little bird, but you mustn't ever fly away!'

Birdy struggled to explain, but when she was back in her cosy bed with Gilbert and Mum gently stroking her shoulder she was suddenly so sleepy she could barely speak.

'Fairy . . . Faraway . . .' she murmured, and then she was fast asleep.

When she woke up there was bright sunshine lighting up the little attic room. She jumped up, ran downstairs and into Milo and Mia's room. They were both still asleep. Milo lay on his back, sprawled like a starfish. The tail of his old dragon toy stuck out from under his quilt. Milo generally tried to keep him hidden. Mia was curled into a little ball, still clutching the book she'd been reading when she went to sleep, *Horse Sense*. She badly wanted horse riding lessons, but Dad said they couldn't afford it. Mia was hoping she might just find a friendly farmer who would let her have a ride on his horse, though she knew it wasn't likely.

'Wake up! We're on holiday! And you'll never ever guess what! I've seen a fairy!' Birdy announced.

Milo raised his head and grunted. Mia put her head under her quilt and mumbled. Birdy frowned at them.

'Didn't you hear what I said? I'VE SEEN A FAIRY!' she shouted.

'Oh, Birdy, it's way too early for pretend games,' Milo said, and Mia threw her pillow at her sister.

'I'm not pretending. I swear I'm not. A big fairy flew straight up to my window. I saw her wings! She wants to meet me at the seaside, far away. Do you think Dad will take us?' Birdy asked, balancing Mia's pillow on her head like a giant squashy hat.

'Go and ask him then,' said Mia, just wanting to get back to sleep.

'Better not,' said Milo, looking at his watch. He

was very proud of it. It was like a real man's watch, big and silver (though it fitted his wrist and it wasn't *real* silver). It told the time accurately and Milo could see it was ten to six – much too early to get up, especially on holiday.

But Birdy scurried off to Mum and Dad's bedroom anyway, using the pillow like a sledge now, punting herself along with her toes. Mum and Dad were cuddled up together, fast asleep.

'Can I come in the cuddle too?' Birdy asked. 'Mum, do you remember, I saw a fairy last night? Dad, can we go to the seaside today? I have to go and see her again!'

They both groaned, which wasn't promising. Mum gave her a telling-off for shunting the pillow around. They let her climb into bed between them though. Dad sleepily explained that the cottage was in the middle of the country and it would take hours and hours to drive to the seaside, and he'd already driven hours and hours to get here yesterday. Mum explained that Birdy hadn't really seen a fairy, she'd just been having a strange dream.

Birdy sighed. 'I absolutely know for sure it wasn't a dream,' she said. 'Why won't anyone believe me?'

She fidgeted rather a lot, fretting about the fairy, desperate to see her again. Dad sighed and dragged himself out of bed.

'Come on, little Miss Wriggle. We'll go downstairs and let Mum have a bit more sleep,' he said wearily.

He made himself a cup of tea and poured Birdy a glass of milk and gave them a biscuit each. Then Birdy sat on Dad's lap and he told her a story about a fairy. It was a good story and normally Birdy would have been thrilled, but she couldn't help feeling irritated. Dad's fairy was tiny and played tricks on people and she wore a dress made of daisies with a buttercup for a hat. She wasn't a bit like the *real* fairy.

After a while Dad's voice slowed and he fell asleep in the middle of a sentence. Birdy wriggled free and went back up to the attic bedroom and peered out of the window just in case the fairy had come back. She looked until her eyes watered and then trailed downstairs again. In the meantime, Dad had gone back up to bed and she could hear him gently snoring now.

Birdy helped herself to another biscuit and suddenly had the idea of making breakfast for everybody. They'd be so pleased and proud of her that she'd done it all by herself. She bustled around setting the table with cups and plates and knives and spoons. She knew Mum and Dad liked tea to drink in the morning, but she also knew she was definitely not allowed to boil the kettle in case it spilt and she burnt herself. They'd have to have milk today. They usually had toast too, but Birdy couldn't find a toaster anywhere, so she simply put a slice of bread on each plate. Luckily it was ready sliced, because using a big sharp knife was totally forbidden too. She could use an ordinary knife though, so she decided to spread everyone's slice for them. She loved spreading. She didn't think Mum or Dad did it properly. She made sure everyone had a really thick yellow layer of butter and then an even thicker layer of raspberry jam. She couldn't stop her fingers delving into the jam several times to give her tongue a thick layer too.

Then she tackled the cornflakes. She carried the milk bottle very carefully on to the table, deciding she'd better not risk pouring it into the jug. Then she reached for the big cornflakes packet. She stood on tiptoe because it was on a high shelf, but she still couldn't reach it. There was an old wooden stool in the corner. She dragged it to the cupboard and stood on it. Just as she took hold of the cornflake packet the stool slipped sideways, one of the legs breaking. Birdy lost her grip. She ended up on her bottom on the floor, while the cornflakes packet wavered, tipped and spilt. Cornflakes showered over the

shelf, and then all over the floor in a golden cascade.

Birdy gave a little scream of woe. She looked round helplessly. Even her slippers were crunching with cornflakes. She started putting them one by one back into the packet, trying not to cry.

'Oh, Birdy!' It was Mum. She must have heard the little scream even though she'd been fast asleep.

'I wanted to make breakfast as a surprise, but it's all gone wrong even though I was being so careful,' Birdy sniffled.

'Oh, well. It *is* a bit of a surprise, even though it's not quite the way you meant it! Don't put the cornflakes back in the packet now they've been on the floor!' said Mum, getting a dustpan and brush. She started sweeping up the cornflakes and putting them in the waste bin.

'We'll have to make do with bread and jam for breakfast this morning,' she said. Then she glanced at the bread Birdy had already prepared.

'Oh, *Birdy!*' she said again. 'You've used up half a pack of butter and nearly all the jam! What am I going to do with you?'

'Sweep me up and put *me* in the waste bin?' Birdy suggested.

'Don't tempt me,' said Mum, but she gave her a comforting cuddle and made sure Birdy hadn't hurt herself.

Luckily when Dad and Milo and Mia came down for breakfast they liked the Birdy bread very much, saying it was extra tasty, so Birdy cheered up completely. When everyone was washed and dressed Birdy tried asking Dad if they could have a trip to a faraway seaside all over again. She could usually wind Dad round her little finger, but this time he just grinned and shook his head.

'I'm not driving anywhere today, poppet. We'll explore the countryside. But first I'd better mend this old stool,' he said.

'And the only driving I'm going to do is to look for a supermarket to stock up on food!' said Mum. 'Anyone want to come with me?'

The children decided they'd sooner stay at the cottage and help Dad mend the stool. He taught carpentry at a college and luckily he had his bag of work tools in the back of the car. He sometimes let Milo and Mia have a go at making things with wood. Birdy was too small and reckless to be allowed anywhere near a hammer and nails. He didn't want to leave her out, so he sent all three children into the garden to play.

It was a pretty garden, with more rose bushes and lavender and pansies and cornflowers and snapdragons, but it was very small and too cramped to play properly. Mia put a snapdragon flower on her finger and made it gently pinch Birdy's nose, which made her laugh – but there were limits to the number of times they could play this game.

They were full of energy after being cooped up in the car all day yesterday. They wanted to run about.

'Perhaps we could run all the way to the sea,' Birdy suggested, ever hopeful.

'Birdy, you'd have to run for weeks before you got there,' Milo puffed. He was running on the spot as fast as he could, thinking wistfully of the sports centre at home and the running track.

There was a small gate at the bottom of the

garden. He opened it and stepped outside, finding himself in a small sandy lane with grass growing here and there. It went on for a long way, towards the wood. He went back into the garden and addressed his father through the open kitchen window.

'Dad, there's a lane out the back, too small for any cars. Could we go out there and race up and down?' he asked.

Dad stopped hammering and went to have a peer himself.

'I suppose so,' he said, a little doubtfully. 'Don't go too far though. Promise?'

'Absolutely!' said Milo. He grinned at his sisters. 'Come on, you lot.'

'I'll come and watch you when I've finished mending this stool, but it's going to take a bit of time. All the legs are wonky, so I might as well fix it properly.'

Milo, Mia and Birdy skipped out of the back gate into the quiet lane. They ran races to the trees where the Enchanted Wood began, letting Mia start a quarter of the way there and Birdy halfway. Milo still won easily. He raised his arms over his head.

'I'm the champion!' he sang.

Mia and Birdy got fed up after the third race.

'Maybe we could just have a little walk in the wood?' Mia suggested. 'I want to see if there are any animals around.'

'Oh, yes, let's!' said Birdy.

'Well, I'd better go and ask Dad,' said Milo, who tried to be very responsible because he was the oldest.

Just then a really big rabbit darted along the ditch, and then stopped still, looking at the children.

'Oh, look!' Mia whispered, not wanting to frighten it away. It was the first time she'd ever seen a rabbit that wasn't cooped up in a hutch.

'Hello, little bunny!' Birdy whispered too, though it almost came up to her knees.

'See how its ears are twitching,' Milo whispered. 'It's listening to us!'

'I *am* listening,' said the rabbit. 'But it's hard to hear exactly what you're saying because you're whispering.'

The three children stood still, their mouths open.

They looked at each other, thinking one of them might be doing a rabbit voice.

'Hello! I'm over here!' said the rabbit.

'Rabbits can't *talk*,' said Milo.

'You said they could, though you were only teasing me,' said Birdy. 'And it is.'

'I suppose Peter Rabbit can talk,' said Mia. 'And Little Grey Rabbit. And the White Rabbit in *Alice's Adventures in Wonderland*.'

'They're not real,' said Milo. 'Maybe this one isn't either. I think we're dreaming.'

'We can't all be having the same dream,' said Mia.

'You're all good at running. But I'm much faster. Bet you can't catch me!' said the rabbit. 'Race you to the Faraway Tree!'

'The Faraway *Tree*!' Birdy gasped, something dawning on her. 'Does a lovely big fairy live there?'

'Yes, that's my friend Silky,' said the rabbit. 'Come *on*!'

He darted up out of the ditch and ran into the Enchanted Wood. And Milo, Mia and Birdy ran after him.

CHAPTER THREE

THEY COULDN'T run very fast in the wood because the trees grew so close together, and their trunks were very thick and gnarled. The knots on the bark looked rather like faces, and the twigs at the end of their branches could be mistaken for long, pointy fingers. Birdy got scratched and stood still, biting her lip.

'Come *on*, Birdy!' said Milo. 'We'll lose sight of the rabbit!'

'I'm not sure I like it here after all. That tree just reached out and grabbed me!' said Birdy. 'And it won't stop looking at me! It's pulling a horrid face!'

'Let's pull a face back,' said Mia.

They made faces back, crossing their eyes, scrunching up their noses and screwing their mouths to one side.

'You're very ugly children!' said the rabbit, darting back.

The tree made a strange rustling noise. The trees nearby did too.

'What's that funny noise?' said Birdy.

'It's just the leaves blowing in the wind,' said Milo.

'But there isn't any wind, not even the slightest breeze,' said Mia.

The three children found they were all holding hands.

'*Wisha-wisha-wisha-wisha-wisha!*' went the trees.

Birdy suddenly brightened. 'Do you know what? I think they're laughing at us!'

The tree branches bobbed up and down and the leaves rustled even louder.

Birdy looked at the tree that had scratched her. The knots on its bark seemed to have rearranged themselves. It looked as if it was grinning now.

Birdy reached out and took hold of a twig. She felt it twitch in her grasp.

'It's shaking hands with me!' she said. 'Oh, you're a friendly tree. Sorry I said you were horrid – you're not a bit!'

'*Wisha-wisha-wisha!*' said the tree, and all the others nearby took up the chorus.

The children set off again after the rabbit. He seemed to be chuckling too. He led them in and out and round the trees, darting down tiny paths, suddenly changing direction altogether. Milo tried to keep track of where they went, but it was impossible.

'Maybe this isn't such a good idea,' he whispered to Mia. He didn't want Birdy to hear in case she worried. 'I think we might get totally lost.'

'No we won't!' said Mia, who could be very bold at times. Or reckless.

'Hello, Mr Tree! Hello, Mrs Tree! Hello, Old Man Tree! Hello, Baby Tree!' Birdy sang, greeting each tree she came across. It sounded quite sweet at first, but then it grew irritating.

'Give it a rest, Birdy,' said Milo. 'Look, the

wood's getting thicker and thicker and I'm not even sure the rabbit knows where it's going. I think we ought to turn back now.'

'Don't be daft!' said Birdy rudely, forgetting that she'd been willing to turn back herself only a few minutes ago. 'We're going to the Faraway Tree to meet my fairy!'

'Nearly there!' said the rabbit, running round them and then rushing off again, his fluffy tail bobbing cheekily.

'I still think...' Milo started, but then he suddenly squinted in the eerie green light of the wood. He saw a little path, wider than the others. It was leading to a trunk – an enormous ancient trunk like a massive wooden tower. The rabbit stood on its hind legs and managed to fold his front ones, a considerable feat for an animal.

'There!' he said triumphantly. 'The Faraway Tree! Though right now it's the Rightinfrontofyoureyes Tree!'

'It's massive!' said Milo, running right round it.

'You really are the most amazing rabbit,' said Mia.

'Where's my fairy, please, Mr Rabbit?' Birdy asked.

'She lives up there,' said the rabbit, pointing his paw up the tree.

'Actually *in* the tree?' said Birdy.

'Several people live there. It's a very exclusive address,' said the rabbit.

'Do *you* live there?' Milo asked, out of breath.

'I'm a rabbit,' he reminded him. 'I live in Sandybank Burrow with my extended family. Speaking of which, a dozen or so of my children and assorted nephews and nieces are at a breakfast party here. We don't let them out at night because of the F-O-X-E-S.'

Birdy looked blank, but Milo and Mia nodded.

'Will you have to climb up to collect them?' Mia asked. She knew rabbits couldn't usually climb, but then they couldn't usually talk either.

'No, no, they will be leaving any minute,' said the rabbit confidently.

At that moment a hidden trapdoor opened at the bottom of the vast tree and several baby rabbits sitting on a cushion shot out, squealing with excitement. They just had time to scamper off the cushion and roll it to one side, when another cluster of small rabbits shot out, and then another and another. They all scampered about, laughing merrily.

'Now, now, calm down!' said the big rabbit, shaking his head at them. 'I'd better get you back to the burrow sharpish, or your mothers will have something to say. Come along!'

They fell into line, still giggling, and he started marching them away, waving his paw to the children. The babies copied him, waving too, though it unbalanced the very little ones and they tumbled sideways. Mia gently set them on all four tiny paws and they scurried away.

Milo was peering into the trapdoor.

'It's like a fantastic slide! Shall we climb up and have a go?' he said to his sisters.

A red squirrel popped out of a hole in the trunk.

'I'm sorry – it's by invitation only,' he said, busy gathering up the cushions.

'You can talk too!' said Mia. 'And you're such a

lovely russet colour. I didn't think there were red squirrels any more, only grey ones.'

'I believe there are some grey newcomers at the edge of the wood,' said the squirrel. But we're all reds round here. My family have been working at the Faraway Tree for many generations. We're cushion gatherers – the best in the business.'

He seized a rope that was slithering down through the branches, tied it neatly round the pile of cushions and tugged three times. The rope rose upwards, taking the cushions with it.

'Who's pulling the rope?' Milo asked, craning his neck as he peered up through the branches.

'My employer, Mr Moonface,' said the squirrel.

'Moonface!' said Milo. 'Has he really got a face like the moon?'

'He's got a very distinguished face,' said the squirrel huffily. 'And I wouldn't peer upwards in that exact spot if I were you. Dame Washalot will have finished her first wash of the day.'

'What do you mean?' said Milo. And then he found out. A waterfall of sudsy warm water suddenly drenched him to the skin. He shrieked. Mia and Birdy cried out too, horrified – and yet Milo looked so bizarre soaking wet they couldn't help laughing too, though they tried not to. The squirrel didn't try not to at all. He laughed so much he fell over, clutching himself.

'Told you!' he said.

'What a horrible, stupid trick!' said Milo, plucking at his dripping T-shirt and shaking his head, so that water sprayed everywhere. He could feel the blood flooding to his face. He hated being laughed at. 'Who is this wretched Washalot person? I'm going to throw water at them and see how they like it!'

'I wouldn't do that if I were you,' said the red squirrel. 'She might try to whack you with her scrubbing brush! Oh, don't be so cross! Look, I've got towels at the ready in case of emergencies.' He put his paw in his cubby hole and brought out a fluffy towel as green as the leaves on the tree.

Milo accepted one rather ungraciously and pulled away when Mia tried to dry him too. He checked his watch to make sure it was all right. It seemed strangely early.

'What time was it when we set out?' he asked Mia.

'Don't know,' she said. 'You're the one with the watch!'

'Do you know what time it is now?' Milo asked the squirrel, though he certainly wasn't wearing a watch either.

'It's daytime,' said the red squirrel, looking surprised. 'Would you like another towel?'

The first towel had been surprisingly absorbent. Milo's hair was nearly dry and his T-shirt and shorts were only slightly damp.

'No thanks,' he said, more politely.

'Come on then, Milo! Let's go and find Silky the fairy. I absolutely love her name!' said Birdy. She jumped up determinedly and managed to swing herself on to the lowest branch, though it was quite a stretch for her.

'Are you sure you're old enough to climb trees, Birdy?' said Milo worriedly.

'Of course I am. It's easy-peasy!' said Birdy,

climbing higher.

'Careful then! Hang on tight. You too, Mia!' said Milo.

'I bet you I'm better at climbing than you are,' said Mia, and leapt up after Birdy.

They'd never climbed a tree before, but both girls did look pretty expert. Milo gritted his teeth and started climbing too. Birdy was right, it was surprisingly easy, though he was careful not to look down. He had never told anyone, but he wasn't too keen on heights.

Milo saw clusters of acorns. That meant it must be an oak tree. When they'd been to the park at home Dad had told him that oak trees could live for hundreds and hundreds of years. This tree certainly seemed astonishingly old, the branches very gnarled – and yet very strong and supportive.

He heard Birdy calling out above him. 'There's a little window in the tree! Oh, this must be where my fairy lives. Silky! Miss Silky Fairy, I'm here!'

Milo pulled himself up the next few branches so quickly he very nearly slipped. Birdy and Mia were peering into a proper latticed window with neat spotted curtains at either side. The window suddenly opened and a cross red face looked out. It belonged to a strange little pixie man, with big, pointy ears and a sharp, pointy nose and an odd, pointy cap on his head.

'Oh, you're not my fairy!' said Birdy, very disappointed.

'Of course I'm not a fairy, you silly little girl! I'm a pixie and I'm sick of being disturbed by nosy children. I'll teach you a lesson!' He reached for a jug on his windowsill.

'Duck!' Milo shouted, realising what he was about to do.

The Angry Pixie threw the jug of water at the two girls. Birdy was so small she was out of reach, but poor Mia got it right in the face. The Angry Pixie nodded in satisfaction and slammed his window shut again.

'You mean, rude, little man!' Mia gasped, blinking.

'Now who looks funny!' said Milo, but he couldn't help feeling sorry for Mia. 'I should have kept hold of that towel.' He gallantly took off his T-shirt and mopped Mia's face.

'We should have brought umbrellas with us today!' said Mia, cheering up.

Milo put his wet T-shirt on again while Birdy went ahead.

'Hey, you two, guess what I've found!' she called.

'If it's a window, keep away from it!' Mia warned.

'It's not a window, it's a door with a little knocker,' said Birdy.

'Don't knock, just in case! Wait for us,' Milo called.

Birdy had found a yellow door at the end of a very broad branch almost like a pathway. It was painted with poppies and bluebells and big daisies, and the polished brass knocker was in the shape of a ladybird.

'Isn't it lovely!' said Birdy. 'I *have* to knock! I just know my Silky fairy lives here.'

She reached up confidently and knocked three times with the ladybird before they could stop her.

'I bet it's where the Washalot woman lives and

I'll get soaked all over again,' said Milo.

But Birdy was right. The door opened and the beautiful fairy stood there, smiling at her. She was wearing a sky-blue dress, very light and floaty, and her shining wings had a pale-blue tint as she opened and closed them excitedly. She danced on the spot, and they saw she'd painted her toenails blue too.

'Oh, I so hoped you'd come to see me!' she said. 'I'm Silky.'

'I'm Birdy! And this is my sister, Mia, and

my brother, Milo,' Birdy said, her voice squeaky with delight.

'Do come in, all of you. I'm preparing lunch!' said Silky.

They went into her tiny house. It was quite dark, but she had strings of little coloured lights all around the room.

'*Fairy* lights!' said Birdy.

Silky had a small blue table studded with mother-of-pearl. The tiny jewels reflected the lights. A glass lamp in the shape of flower petals glowed in the corner. There were several small chairs with blue velvet upholstery, a neat little bed with a pink and blue satin coverlet, and a small stove and a cupboard painted with flowers like the door outside. She had a mantelpiece with gleaming blue vases on either end. A surprisingly large clock stood in the middle with a smiley face. It had big eyes that slanted to the left when it ticked, and to the right when it tocked. The children stared at it, moving their own eyes in time.

'I love your funny clock!' said Milo.

'I love your pearly table,' said Mia.

'I love everything! Your room's absolutely beautiful!' said Birdy, clasping her hands in awe.

Silky smiled proudly and told them to sit down while she cooked.

'I do hope you like cheesy pancakes,' she said, a little anxiously.

'We love them,' said Milo, relieved. He'd wondered if fairies ate food like nectar or rose petals, and he wasn't sure he'd like that sort of meal. He realised he was starving hungry, which wasn't surprising after getting soaked and then climbing halfway up the biggest tree in the wood.

'Can we help with anything?' Mia asked politely. She'd heard Mum say that when they were visiting. She and Milo were no better at cookery than Birdy, but she felt she'd better offer.

'Perhaps you could set the table for me?' said Silky, throwing a white cloth embroidered with bluebells over her pearly table. She showed Mia where the blue china was neatly stored. 'And could one of you pop outside and pick several peaches, please? They're perfectly ripe today. I think fresh peach juice is delicious, don't you?'

She gave Milo a big basin to carry them in.

'*Pick* them?' said Milo. How could you possibly pick peaches from an oak tree? But when he went outside he saw some of the slender branches above were laden with rosy yellow peaches. He picked four, putting them very gently in the basin so that they didn't bruise. When he went indoors again Silky showed him how to use the fruit squeezer.

Silky asked Mia if she'd grate the cheese. Mia was a little worried she might grate her hand too, but she got the hang of it immediately.

'Can't I have a go?' Birdy asked, desperate to help as well.

'I rather hoped you'd help me beat the batter, Birdy,' said Silky.

'Oh, yes please!' said Birdy.

Milo and Mia looked at each other, wondering if she'd beat too enthusiastically and spatter the beautiful blue room, but Silky put her cool hands over Birdy's hot ones and showed her exactly how to beat.

'It's beautifully smooth now,' said Silky. 'Now for the fun part! We'll make your pancake first, shall we, Birdy?'

Silky poured the batter into sizzling butter in the frying pan on the stove. When she judged it was cooked on one side she tossed the pancake. It went high in the air, circled the entire ceiling twice and then flipped itself over and landed neatly back in the butter.

'How did you *do* that?' asked Mia. She was proud that she'd learnt to throw a ball properly with a flick of the wrist, but Silky's skill was something else altogether.

'It's just a little knack,' said Silky modestly. She set the first pancake on a blue plate in front of Birdy, with a glass of peach juice to wash it down.

'Eat up before it gets cold,' said Silky, starting the next pancake.

It was the most heavenly pancake in the world, light and golden and deliciously cheesy. Milo and

Mia waited for theirs, mouths watering. Silky made her own pancake last, eating daintily, and then smiled.

'Shall we have dessert now?' she said.

'Yes please!' said the children.

Silky took a big blue tin from her larder. She set it on the table. It immediately revolved slowly round and round, while a tune tinkled prettily.

'It's a musical tin! Our mum once had a box of biscuits like that,' said Mia.

Silky took the lid off the tin and they peered

inside. It wasn't full of biscuits. It held four little round sponge cakes covered with white icing and sprinkled with rainbow dots and silver balls. They were all spinning round too, and humming in time to the tune.

'Magic fairy cakes!' said Birdy.

'Choose which one you want,' said Silky.

They looked absolutely identical, but it was fun choosing all the same. As soon as they picked a cake, the icing changed colour. Milo's went red, Mia's went brown, Birdy's went purple – but Silky's cake stayed white.

'Why hasn't yours changed colour, Silky?' Milo asked.

'Mine is vanilla, with cream, my favourite,' said Silky.

The cakes still spun round as the children picked them up, so they had to grip each one tightly and aim carefully when taking a bite. They got icing and buttercream all round their mouths and cheeks. Birdy even got cream in her ears. They didn't mind at all!

Milo discovered that his cake was a wonderful strawberry flavour. Mia's cake was chocolate and Birdy's blackcurrant. They ate in blissful silence while the tin stayed whirling, playing a medley of tunes, and the clock ticked in time. Its hands revolved this way and that, as if it were swinging its arms. It wasn't telling the time properly at all.

Milo watched it – and then his heart started thudding. He peered at his own watch. It was still stuck at ten o'clock. It must have stopped when he got soaked by the washing water. He tried shaking it and fiddling with the catch, but the hands stayed still. He tried to work out the time in his head. They must have been gone an hour. Maybe two hours? Dad would be out looking for them, desperately worried. Mum would be back from the shops, horrified that the children were missing. They were going to be in serious trouble!

CHAPTER FOUR

'Do YOU happen to know the actual time, Silky?' he asked.

She looked surprised. 'Not really. It can be any time you wish here in the Faraway Tree. Are you sleepy now, after your meal? Would you like it to be bedtime?'

'No! But whatever time it is, we're very late! We have to go back home straight away!' said Milo, standing up.

'Oh, Milo, don't be silly. We're having such a lovely time with Silky,' said Mia.

'I want to stay here till it really is bedtime!'

said Birdy.

As if to oblige her the clock suddenly started chiming eight o'clock, her actual bedtime. Then it paused, pleased with itself, and started chiming all over again, all the way up to twelve – and then thirteen, and fourteen, and fifteen.

'Dad will have been looking for us for ages! And Mum will be back from the shops! They'll be so worried!' Milo said urgently, shouting above the din.

'Oh, help,' said Mia. 'You're right!'

'But I still want to stay with Silky,' said Birdy.

Silky smiled at her. 'You can come back and see me another time, dear Birdy.'

'Tomorrow?' Birdy asked.

'And the day after that, and the day after that,' said Silky. 'But you'd better go home now if your parents will be worrying.'

'I don't think they'll be worrying *just* yet,' said Birdy, still sitting down.

'Birdy, don't be silly!' said Milo sharply.

'Come on!' said Mia, pulling Birdy up and dragging her to the door. She didn't really mean to be rough with her, she was just panicking, but Birdy objected strongly.

'Ouch! You're twisting my arm! Stop it!' said Birdy and started to cry. 'Silky, please, please, please let me stay with you!'

'Stop behaving like a spoilt baby,' Mia hissed in her ear, but she rubbed her arm just in case she really had hurt her.

'Mum and Dad will never let us go out in the lane again!' said Milo. 'Quick! Down the tree! I'm so sorry to be rude, Silky.'

'Thank you very much for our lovely lunch,' Mia gabbled, steering Birdy to the door by her shoulders. 'Say thank you to Silky, Birdy.'

'But I don't want to go!' Birdy wept.

'Start climbing down *now*!' Milo commanded.

Birdy dangled one leg, sobbing. She looked down. And down and down and down.

'I can't! It's too scary!' she said. 'I'm too little.'

'Don't try and pull that one! I thought you said climbing trees was easy-peasy,' Mia said sternly, trying to help her.

'Stop pushing me!' Birdy shrieked. 'Climbing *up* trees is easy. Climbing *down* is awful.'

Milo was looking down too. He secretly agreed with her. He started shaking, praying no one would notice. Even fearless Mia was looking a bit wobbly.

'Don't worry, there's a much quicker way of getting down the tree,' said Silky helpfully. 'Follow me.'

She started climbing *up* the tree, barely skimming it, her wings outspread. Birdy stopped crying, watching in awe.

'But we need to go *down*, Silky,' said Milo.

'You will be down in just a tick, I promise,' said Silky. 'I'm taking you to meet my friend Moonface. He'll let you go down his slippery-slip.'

'Oh!' said Milo. 'That slide thing! And we'll pop out right at the bottom of the tree! Brilliant!'

'He usually asks for toffee or chocolate as payment – he's got a very sweet tooth. But don't worry, I'll give him one of my fairy cakes,' Silky called down. 'I'll make a new batch for tea.'

She was already at another small door in the tree, rapping with the silver knocker. She had to rap hard several times before the door opened. A strange little man peered out. He had a very natty style of dressing, wearing a beautifully cut scarlet jacket, a canary-yellow waistcoat, tight checked trousers and a big spotty bow tie – but the most distinctive thing about him was his big round white face, like a full moon.

'Silky, my dear!' he said, smiling. He peered around her at the children. 'And some new friends!'

'Milo, Mia and dear little Birdy. They're desperate to get home, Moonface dear. Could they possibly use your slippery-slip? I'll take care of their payment with a fairy cake,' said Silky. 'Banana flavour – your favourite.'

'Perhaps three cakes, one for each child? I'm also very fond of caramel – and your lemon cakes are deliciously refreshing,' said Moonface, licking his lips.

'Really, Moonface! You won't be able to button your waistcoat soon,' said Silky. 'Can we discuss the cakes later, when the children are safely home?'

'Oh, very well,' said Moonface, sighing. 'Come in then. I'm afraid my room is in rather a mess.'

The room itself was delightful, as round as Moonface's head, with carved wooden furniture curved all the way round a large hole in the floor, partitioned with a little curved wall so one couldn't step down it by accident. But the round patterned carpet was covered with marbles and spinning tops and a hundred and two Noah's ark wooden animals and the ark itself and Mr Noah and his family, and a sea of sweet wrappers and empty bottles of pop and nibbled biscuits and cake crumbs. His small stove was a mess of used saucepans and spilt milk, and his tiny sink was piled high with plates and cups and saucers, on the brink of overbalancing.

'Oh, Moonface!' said Silky, sighing deeply. 'I only cleaned your room yesterday and now look at it!'

Mia blinked in astonishment.

'Don't blame me, Silky! It was all those rabbit children. We were having a little party,' said Moonface.

'You're the biggest child of all!' said Silky. 'Once I've helped these children get home I suppose I shall have to come back and start cleaning all over again. Which means there will be no time at all for cake making! And it serves you right!'

Milo was astonished. Mia was angry.

'Why on earth should it be Silky's job to clean up after you, Mr Moonface?' she said. 'It's terribly old-fashioned to expect a woman to keep a house tidy, especially when it's not even hers. My mum and dad share all the chores, and we have to help too.'

Birdy couldn't be bothered with household responsibilities. She waded through the litter and took Silky's hand.

'Will you come to my window tonight and wave to me again?' she begged.

'Yes, I always have a little fly-about after supper to stretch my wings,' she said. 'Of course I shall wave to you, Birdy. Now, who's going first down naughty Moonface's slippery-slip?' She went to a pile of higgledly-piggledy cushions. Several were leaking feathers. 'I do believe you've had a cushion fight, Moonface! Really!'

'I'll go down first! Please!' said Mia.

Silky selected an orange cushion for her, and Moonface opened a little door in the wall around the slippery-slip. There was a smooth ledge at the top where Mia could set her cushion and sit on it.

'Ready?' said Moonface.

'You bet!' said Mia.

He gave her a gentle push and she flew downwards, going round and round and round, screaming in delight. It was very dark and the ride seemed to be going on for ever, but Mia adored it. She suddenly shot out of the trapdoor right at the bottom of the tree, landing on a patch of thick, soft grass. She lay back on her cushion, laughing delightedly.

The red squirrel scurried over to her.

'Up you get!' he said. 'Cushion please! You don't want the others to land on top of you.'

There was a short delay. Birdy had gone next after Mia, but when she sat on the ledge on her crimson cushion she looked down at the seemingly endless dark hole below her.

'I can't!' she whispered.

Milo saw she was genuinely frightened.

'We'll share a cushion. You sit on my lap, Birdy. It'll be fun,' he said.

He wasn't too sure himself, but he was trying to be brave – and he was desperate to get back to the cottage. He sat on the cushion, Birdy sat on top of him and Moonface gave them a push. They went swooping down, faster and faster and faster. Birdy yelled, but it was with sudden amazing joy. Her curly hair was tickling Milo's nose and she was surprisingly heavy for such a small girl, but he loved the ride too. It was better than any slide in a playground, better than any helter-skelter at a fair, better than anything he'd ever experienced in his life – and when they shot out of the trapdoor at the bottom of the Faraway Tree all he wanted to do was climb right up it and have another go.

But he knew they had to get back as soon as possible to stop their poor parents being worried. The only trouble was that they weren't sure which way to go. They'd followed the rabbit all the way, and the paths were so twisty and confusing that they didn't know *which* way.

'Follow me!' a voice called from above.

It was Silky, flying low down, her wings spread wide, her long hair billowing behind her. She guided them all the way through the wood, cleverly ducking branches and circling trees while they caught up with her. It wasn't long before the trees thinned out and they found themselves back at the little ditch and the small sandy lane.

Silky waved and flew off in a flash before they even had time to thank her. The children took deep breaths, plucking up the courage to return to the cottage. They imagined Dad distraught, Mum crying. They pictured their sudden joy and relief when they saw the children. And then even more vividly they imagined their anger when they realised the children had gone into the Enchanted Wood and had scarcely given their parents a thought for hours.

'They didn't actually forbid us to go there,' Mia said.

'Come off it, Mia. You know perfectly well Dad thought we'd just be playing races in the lane,' said Milo.

'It's my fault,' Birdy said miserably. 'I just wanted to see my fairy. And I'm so glad I did! But I don't want Mum and Dad to be cross with me.'

They trailed back to the little gate and let themselves in. The garden was empty. The kitchen window was open and they heard Dad singing away to himself as he hammered. They peered at each other, bewildered. Hadn't Dad even noticed they were missing? And where was Mum?

They ran indoors. Dad was busy hammering a nail and didn't even look up.

'Hi, kids,' he said casually. 'Have you got fed up with racing already?'

Already? There was an old-fashioned cuckoo clock hanging on the kitchen wall. They peered at the time. Birdy hadn't quite mastered how to tell the time, but even she could tell they seemed to have been out in the lane for a matter of minutes. Milo looked at his watch, baffled. It was going again now, but it was only saying it was ten past ten. How was that possible?

It was Mia who worked it out first.

'The Enchanted Wood doesn't have any proper time. Remember Silky's clock? So we can spend all day there if we want and Mum and Dad will think we've just popped out for five minutes!' she whispered, as they left Dad to his hammering.

'Magic!' said Milo.

'It *is* magic!' said Birdy. 'So I can go and see Silky any time I like and I won't ever get into trouble with Mum and Dad? Let's go back to the Enchanted Wood right this minute! I didn't have time to say goodbye to Silky properly.'

'We didn't even say thank you properly,' said Mia.

'And now she'll be making her fairy cakes for Moonface,' said Birdy.

'Banana, caramel and lemon,' said Milo, licking his lips. 'We didn't even say thank you to Moonface and yet he let us use his slippery-slip.'

'Tell you what – let's tear two pages out of my drawing book and write them proper thank-you letters,' Mia suggested. 'Grown-ups always like them.'

'*Are* they grown-ups?' said Birdy. 'They're only as big as us.'

'I suppose if they're magic they can be any size they want,' said Milo. 'It doesn't matter a bit if you're not very tall.'

He was very conscious of the fact that Mia was nearly as tall as he was, though she was nearly two years younger.

'Can't we do the thank-you cards later and go back to the Enchanted Wood *now*?' said Birdy.

It was very tempting, but just then Dad came out of the kitchen carrying a mug of hot chocolate for each of them, with whipped cream on top *and* a marshmallow, and he stayed chatting to them because he'd finished mending the stool. Then he suggested playing a game of French cricket in the back lane.

This was great fun, but it was tantalising to see

the Enchanted Wood so nearby. Birdy kept glancing at it longingly.

'Couldn't we go for a walk in the wood now, Dad?' she asked.

Milo and Mia looked at each other, alarmed. They hadn't discussed it, but they both knew they wanted to keep the Faraway Tree and the strange folk that lived there a secret. Dad was great fun and sometimes joined in their games, but they couldn't imagine him chatting to a fairy or sliding down Moonface's slippery-slip. They were pretty certain he wouldn't let them climb up the tree in the first place, especially Birdy.

They frowned at her now, trying to make her shut up by sheer willpower – but Dad wasn't keen on the idea anyway.

'Mum will wonder where we are when she comes back,' he said. 'I'm not sure you could actually walk through the wood anyway. It looks as if the trees grow far too thickly.'

'That's right,' said Milo quickly, while Mia mouthed at Birdy, *It's a secret!*

'Oh, look!' Dad suddenly whispered. 'There's a rabbit in the ditch!'

They all held their breath, but the rabbit didn't pause. It just scurried past without saying a word, like any normal rabbit, to their relief. Birdy couldn't help whispering after it, 'If you know her, say hello to Silky for me!'

'Who's Silky?' Dad asked.

'She's my friend. She's a fairy!' Birdy said proudly, before Milo and Mia could stop her.

But Dad just looked amused. 'A *fairy*?' he said, in the special fond tone he had for Birdy. 'Oh, how lovely. Can she give you magic wishes? Let's wish Mum comes home quickly and then we can go out exploring.'

It was clear he thought Birdy was making it all up. Mum came back with all kinds of goodies from the village shop. While she was unpacking the bags and having a cup of coffee with Dad the children went to Milo and Mia's bedroom and dutifully wrote their thank-you cards.

Milo drew a big tree with lots of little doors and

windows, with Silky and Moonface peering out, smiling. He wrote, 'Thank you very much for a lovely time. Best wishes from Milo.'

Mia drew herself swooping down the slippery-slip, her mouth wide open with joy. She wrote, 'Thank you for a magic day. Love from Mia.'

Birdy concentrated very hard on her picture, the tip of her tongue hanging out as she drew a picture of Silky and Moonface. He was quite easy for her to draw, because she just did a big round head with stick arms and legs coming out of it. Silky was much harder, because Birdy wanted to make her look beautiful. She commandeered Mia's yellow felt pen and nearly used up all the ink giving Silky long hair right down to her ankles. Her face was much too pink and her wings were lopsided. Birdy despaired, but Mia was kind and told her she'd drawn a beautiful picture. She even managed a message. 'I luv yoo from Birdy.'

Then they went for a long walk with Mum and Dad and had a picnic lunch on the top of a hill. They could see the Enchanted Wood – but all the trees looked far away now, and the Faraway Tree itself was hidden by a big cloud.

Dad spotted a river gleaming in the sunshine.

'Look, Birdy! I can't take you to a faraway sea, but will a faraway river do instead?'

Birdy wasn't usually the most tactful person, but she knew Dad was trying hard to please her, so she said yes, it looked lovely. They went back to the cottage to the car and drove to the river, and it *was* lovely, with shallow parts where the children could paddle, though it was icy cold at first. Milo tried to catch a fish with his bare hands and Mia spotted two frogs and Birdy found a shiny green stone that she thought might be an emerald. But it wasn't magical, like the Faraway Tree.

Dad asked them what they'd like for tea and Birdy suggested cheesy pancakes. Dad was surprised because he'd never cooked them savoury pancakes before, but he was happy to have a go. He tossed them properly too, but his pancakes just flipped up from the pan and down again – they didn't fly all round the ceiling. They were very tasty, but they weren't as good as Silky's.

'Shall we go out to the lane and play races again?' Milo said after tea, winking at Mia and Birdy.

But their hopes of sneaking off were thwarted. Mum and Dad played French cricket with them in the back garden, and when it started to get a bit chilly they all went indoors and played Happy Families. It was fun, but nowhere near as exciting as jumping over the ditch, threading their way through the wood and finding the Faraway Tree.

Then it was bedtime. Birdy usually protested, but practically shot up the stairs this time. She let herself be tucked up by Mum and Dad, and then jumped out of bed again the moment they'd gone down the little stairs to kiss Milo and Mia goodnight. She waited by the window, staring out into the twilight until her eyes watered.

Then she saw a glowing light in the distance. It got nearer and nearer, until she could make out a gleam of golden hair, a shimmer of pearly wings. Birdy's heart beat faster.

'Silky!' she whispered.

A NEW ADVENTURE

Silky flew right up to the small window, reaching out her hand. Birdy reached out too, and they both touched the glass together.

'See you tomorrow?' Silky mouthed.

'Tomorrow!' said Birdy.

She went to sleep murmuring, 'Tomorrow! Tomorrow! Tomorrow!'

CHAPTER FIVE

THE CHILDREN managed to escape straight after breakfast. Mum and Dad were still in their night clothes, having a second pot of coffee together. Milo hid the three thank-you pictures up inside his T-shirt.

'We'll just be outside in the lane,' said Milo, as casually as he could. 'Racing.'

'You're taking your running very seriously, son,' said Dad proudly.

'So am I. I can very nearly beat him,' said Mia.

'And so can I,' said Birdy, telling a shameless fib.

Mum and Dad smiled fondly. The children ran

out into the garden, out of the gate and along the lane.

'Keep running for a bit,' said Milo. 'Just in case Mum and Dad are watching. And then it'll mean I haven't told a lie because we really have been racing.'

So they charged up and down for two minutes.

'Can't we go to see Silky *now*?' Birdy puffed. 'We've been running for at least an hour!'

'Come on then,' said Mia.

She took Birdy's hand, Milo took the other, and all three jumped right over the ditch into the Enchanted Wood. The trees went *wisha-wisha-wisha* as if they were greeting them. They looked hard for the magic talking rabbit, but they couldn't see him anywhere. Once or twice Mia spotted a fluffy white tail in the distance, but it always disappeared long before they could reach it.

'But look!' Mia whispered, suddenly awestruck.

There was a small brown fawn trotting between the trees, its back dappled with pretty white spots. It was looking directly at them, its big brown eyes

gentle. It approached until it was standing right in front of them.

They stood very still, though Birdy was so excited she wanted to hop up and down.

'Are you looking for the Faraway Tree?' it said, so softly they had to strain their ears.

'Yes, we are, little fawn,' said Mia, very quietly.

'Could you possibly take us there?' Milo whispered.

'Oh, please, please, please!' said Birdy.

'Then follow me,' said the fawn, and it turned

round and set off so nimbly they had to trot to keep up.

'Oh, joy!' said Mia. 'It's a fallow deer, because of its markings.'

'It's a *magic* deer because of its speech!' said Milo.

'Do you think it might let me ride on its back?' Birdy asked.

'Of course not – you're much too big!' said Mia.

Birdy sighed. She was usually told she was too little, but now she was too big. She never seemed to be the right size. She was actually finding it quite hard to keep up, and once she blundered into a patch of nettles which stung her bare legs. She would normally have made a great deal of fuss, maybe even cried, but she wanted to see Silky so badly she decided to grit her teeth and put up with the pain.

By the time they got to the wonderful Faraway Tree one of her legs was scarlet with stings.

'Oh, Birdy, your poor leg!' said Milo, suddenly noticing.

'We'll look for a dock leaf. If we rub it on your

leg, it will soothe it,' said Mia.

'Perhaps I could help make it better?' said the fawn humbly. It came right up to Birdy, bent its beautiful head and very gently licked her leg with its long tongue.

Birdy gave a little cry at its soft, raspy feel, but almost immediately the sting eased. The fawn licked a while longer and the angry red stings faded right away.

'Thank you *so* much!' said Birdy, giving the fawn a grateful stroke. 'You've made it completely better!'

'You're very welcome,' said the fawn, and then trotted away happily.

'That's so weird!' said Milo. 'Do you think deer saliva has got some special healing powers? Maybe we've made a brilliant new scientific discovery!'

'It's not *all* deer, just magic ones in the Enchanted Wood, silly,' said Mia. She was a little rattled that the deer had licked Birdy and not her.

'Come *on*,' said Birdy impatiently. 'Let's get climbing!'

She pulled herself up on to the first branch and

the others followed. They came to the Angry Pixie's window. He was watering a potted plant on the windowsill with a small jug. He heard the children and peered out at them, looking very fierce.

'No peeping!' he said furiously.

'You're the one peeping at us!' said Milo.

'Watch out!' said Mia, but she was too late with her warning.

The pixie opened his window wide in a flash and threw the water in his jug right in Milo's face.

'Serves you right!' he said, and slammed the window shut again.

'For goodness' sake!' Milo spluttered, shaking his head like a wet dog.

'Don't get our thank-you cards wet!' said Mia, quickly rescuing them from under his T-shirt.

'I'm not going to bother washing before we come to the Faraway Tree,' said Milo. 'The folk here are determined to do it for me!'

He kept looking up nervously, wondering if Dame Washalot was going to empty her washing tub all over him too. As they reached Silky's branch

he heard a sudden trickle of water up above, and had time to duck, pulling his sisters with him. Birdy got her shoes a little splashed, but the water was cooling on her stung leg, and she was so eager to see Silky that she barely noticed anyway.

She knocked at the flowery door and Silky flung it wide. She had a different dress on today, a beautiful pale primrose yellow. She had somehow managed to change the colour of her wings, so that they were primrose too, with the under feathers a darker daffodil shade.

She greeted them joyfully and gave each child a hug.

'I'm so glad you came! I do hope your parents weren't too worried yesterday,' she said.

'They weren't worried at all! Milo was silly making us hurry back so quickly,' said Birdy.

'I think he was just being responsible,' said Silky. 'I wish I had a kind big brother like Milo.'

Milo positively glowed.

'Moonface is a bit like a brother to you, isn't he?' Mia suggested.

'Like a very *trying* brother!' said Silky. 'I spent ages tidying his home yesterday and he promised to mend his ways. Well ha, ha! He came knocking at my door this morning complaining that he couldn't find his favourite jacket and wondering if I'd borrowed it. As if I'd want to wear it! Anyway, I went up to help him find it and discovered he'd tipped every single item in his wardrobe all over the floor. It was knee-deep in clothes! And when I eventually found his jacket for him it was tumbled up in his bedclothes. He'd worn it while sitting up in bed last night reading his book of magic spells.'

'Moonface can do magic?' Mia asked excitedly.

'Well, he's only on *Book Two* – still quite simple stuff,' said Silky. 'If you've got any warts, I expect he could cure them – or he can charm a bat out of your hair if it happens to get tangled there.'

'I don't think we've got any warts or tangled bats,' said Milo.

'Can *you* do magic, Silky?' Birdy asked.

Silky sighed. 'I'm sure I *could*, but the Enchanted Wood is a very backwards, old-fashioned place.

Girls are only taught domestic skills at Enchanter School. Imagine!'

'But girls are just as clever as boys,' said Mia indignantly. 'Sometimes cleverer!'

'Still, you can make flying pancakes and fairy cakes that go round and round,' said Birdy.

'They're *very* magical,' said Milo, remembering his manners. He remembered their thank-you cards too, and shyly produced them. They were a little crumpled and damp at the edges, but Silky was delighted.

'They're so beautiful!' she said. 'I've never ever had a thank-you card before, and now I've got three of them.'

'They're for Moonface too,' said Birdy. 'But mine's mostly for you, Silky.'

'Well, we'll pop up the tree to show him – but I think it'll make more sense if I display them on my mantelpiece,' said Silky. 'Moonface's is crowded with old spell bottles and slippery oil for his slide and old packets of cereal and jars of jam because he keeps his larder in such a mess.'

They made their way up the tree, Silky politely climbing too, though she could have flown upwards in five seconds. They knocked on Moonface's door and he answered it, closing the door behind him.

'Ah, Milo, Mia and Birdy, how lovely to see you. And you too, Silky, of course,' he said, but he looked a bit wary now. There was a strange, high-pitched chattering sound coming from inside his house.

'The children have made us some beautiful thank-you cards, Moonface,' said Silky, showing him.

'Ah, delightful, how very kind and polite,' said Moonface, looking at them.

'Aren't you going to ask us in?' said Silky.

'Well, my room's a little crowded right now. I have an entire class of nursery squirrels here on a school trip and I have to keep them under the strictest supervision so they don't all try to dive down the slippery-slip at once,' said Moonface.

'Baby squirrels!' said Mia. 'Oh, please, could we just have a look at them?'

'Oh, very well,' said Moonface. 'They are very sweet, if a tad overexcited. Come in, you three. Silky,

84

perhaps you'd like to stay outside – I'm afraid there's no room for you. You're a bit too big.'

Silky was the most slender of fairies and took up far less room than any of the children or indeed Moonface himself, so this was clearly ridiculous. She sighed.

'Have you got your room in a mess again, Moonface?' she said.

'No, no! My clothes are all hanging up in my wardrobe just as you left them,' said Moonface, but he was careful not to say that the room itself was tidy.

It was clear why when he rather reluctantly opened the door. It was complete chaos. Little squirrels in green blazers were scampering everywhere, swarming all over the sofa, even hanging from the pictures on his round walls, their tails waving. They jumped into the cupboards, pulling out every item and dropping them on the floor. Two squirrels were in the process of emptying the wastepaper basket and another pair were yanking all the books from the shelves. They were all talking at once in high, squeaky voices – which rose even higher when they saw Milo, Mia and Birdy.

'*Children! Real children! Wow!*' they marvelled, as if they were rare mythical creatures.

Mia crouched down to talk to them, but knelt on something small and hard that dug into her knee. It was an acorn.

'What on earth are you doing, squirrels?' Silky shouted. 'Moonface, why are you letting them wreck your entire room?'

'I just thought they'd enjoy a game of Hunt the Acorn,' said Moonface, hanging his large round head. 'Every time a squirrel finds one I give them a Toffee Shock as a reward.'

'It's such fun!' said the squirrels, bouncing up and down in delight.

'You're hopeless, Moonface,' said Silky, sighing.

'What's a Toffee Shock?' Milo asked.

'Ah, my little speciality snack!' said Moonface, reaching for a tin. The squirrels squeaked eagerly, smacking their lips. 'I think you've all managed to win one already. I'm just going to give one each to the children.'

'Do they eat real food, just like us?' said a squirrel, and they all giggled together as if it was the funniest idea.

Moonface handed the tin round to the children and they each took a toffee. They were very small, about the size of a thumbnail, so they looked as if they'd be gone in a couple of chews. Still they tasted absolutely delicious – very buttery and sweet.

'You have a Toffee Shock too, Silky,' said Moonface. 'In fact take two, my dearest friend. Take a whole handful to nibble later.'

'You're just trying to get around me, so I'll tidy up all over again,' said Silky, but she was very fond of Moonface even so – and very fond of his special toffees too. She took one and Moonface beamed. He couldn't bear it when Silky was cross with him, though it didn't make him try to be tidier.

Silky chewed happily, knowing what was going to happen next. Milo and Mia and Birdy chewed. The Toffee Shocks seemed doubly delicious. *Trebly* delicious. They coated their tongues and stuck to their teeth. It wasn't a tiny little toffee any more. It grew the more they chewed. It felt as if they had a whole slab of toffee in their mouths. Small drools of toffee dribbled down their chins, as they struggled to speak. They couldn't manage words, only able to make an *ooble-ooble-ooble* sound. Then just as the toffee seemed as big as a balloon it suddenly made a loud popping sound and burst, leaving just a lovely caramel taste.

'Oh my goodness, that's the best toffee *ever*!' said Milo.

'It's fantastic, Moonface!' said Mia, licking her lips.

'*Ooble-ooble-ooble!*' said Birdy, who didn't chew as fast as the others. Then her Toffee Shock burst too, and she looked so astonished the others couldn't help laughing.

The squirrels all started giggling too, and began hunting for hidden acorns again, desperate to win more Toffee Shocks for themselves. They even wondered if Moonface had an acorn or two hidden about his person, so they swarmed all over him, scrabbling in his pockets with their sticky little paws.

'Stop it, you're tickling!' Moonface laughed, trying to bat them away.

'I think it's about time they had their ride down the slippery-slip,' Silky suggested.

'But they're all having such fun!' Moonface protested, not seeming to mind that they were patterning his shirt and jacket with toffee stains.

'Oh, dear, I've got toffee all down my dress!' said Birdy. She usually wore T-shirts and shorts on holiday, but she'd wanted to wear her best dress to impress Silky today. She'd had quite an argument about it with Mum before she got her own way.

'Mum might be a bit cross,' she said, rubbing at the stain, but only making it worse.

'Don't worry – I know someone who'll sort your dress out for you,' said Silky. 'Come on – we'll go and visit her.'

'Is she another fairy?' Birdy asked eagerly.

'No, she's a lady. Dame Washalot,' said Silky.

'Oh, *her*,' said Milo.

'A dame like in a pantomime?' Mia asked.

Dame Washalot did look rather like a pantomime dame when they met her further up the tree. She had a funny mob cap and a long purple dress with the sleeves rolled up, a big white apron, red and black striped stockings and pointy buckled shoes. She had a big wooden washing tub carefully balanced on the broadest part of the branch outside her house and was up to her elbows in soapy water, scrubbing away at her washing.

'Dame Washalot, I wonder if you could help my friend Birdy here clean her dress?' Silky asked politely.

'But please don't throw your water over her. She's only small. You drenched me yesterday, and it was horrible!' said Milo.

'Nonsense!' said Dame Washalot briskly. 'I gave you a free shower, you cheeky boy! You should be grateful that I cleaned you up.'

'But I wasn't grubby!' Milo protested.

'But Birdy is, just a little,' Silky said gently. 'Do you think you could be a darling, Dame Washalot, and give her pretty dress a magic wash?'

Dame Washalot sniffed, but she had a very soft spot for Silky.

'Take your dress off, child,' she said to Birdy.

Birdy looked taken aback.

'Couldn't you just give the stained part a bit of a wipe?' Mia asked.

'My name is Dame Washalot, *not* Dame Bitofawipe,' Dame Washalot said firmly.

Birdy struggled out of her dress reluctantly, feeling a little foolish standing there on the branch in her knickers.

'Could it possibly be a super-speedy magic wash?'

Silky asked Dame Washalot.

'I suppose so, though it takes up an awful lot of energy. I'm not getting any younger, Silky!' she said,

but she dipped Birdy's dress into the blue soapy water in her tub. She took a deep breath and then started scrubbing – but so quickly they couldn't even see her hands they were moving so fast. Water flew from the tub in a fine spray, so the children had to step back. Then Dame Washalot dowsed Birdy's dress in another tub of clean water, whirling it around at the speed of light, and then held it up in the air and waved it wildly like a flag. The wet dress changed from soaking to damp to bone dry without a single crease in seconds, and Dame Washalot handed it over to Birdy with a flourish.

'Marvellous!' said Silky, clapping her performance.

The children clapped too, even Milo. He helped Birdy put her dress back on. It smelt clean and fresh, and the toffee stains had all vanished.

'That was wonderful,' he said, impressed. 'You're better than the best washing machine in the world.'

'*I* am a washing machine,' said Dame Washalot grandly.

'Do we need to pay you?' Mia asked worriedly, because they didn't have any money with them

'The folk of the Faraway Tree usually pay me in fruit and nuts currency,' said Dame Washalot. She

93

peered at the branches. 'Aha! I'll have a nice big bunch of bananas, please.'

'Bananas?' Milo muttered. He knew bananas couldn't possibly grow on trees in this country – but when he looked up he saw bunches of yellow curved fruit right above his head.

He picked the biggest bunch of all and handed them over to Dame Washalot with a little bow. She smiled graciously in a royal way, as if her white mop cap was a golden crown, and waved farewell.

The children picked a bunch of bananas for themselves, and then sat on a branch swinging their legs enjoying them.

'What's that funny noise?' said Birdy, who had sharp ears.

They all listened. It was a very snorty sort of noise, which made them all giggle.

'I think it's Mr Watzisname snoring,' Silky said.

'Mr Watzisname?' they said.

'He's got a very strange, complicated name and even he can't quite remember what it is,' said Silky. 'And I daresay his friend the Saucepan Man will be having a snooze with him. Do you want to have a peep?'

There were two small, elderly gentlemen on the next branch along, lying in deckchairs, comfy cushions under their heads. Mr Watzisname seemed like some sort of gnome, with a red cap and very big, pointy ears. His sleeves were rolled up and his waistcoat was undone. The Saucepan Man had one eye open, his ruddy face beaming at them. He wore the most extraordinary selection of saucepans strung all over his small person, and even had one on top of his head.

'Visitors!' he said, and then he started rapping, drumming out the rhythm on his two front saucepans.

'Two men who are sleeping,
Two fairies who fly,
Two children who're peeping,
With a hi-tiddle-hi!'

The children laughed, but Birdy was puzzled. She couldn't always count accurately, but even she knew the Saucepan Man had got it wrong.

'You said two fairies, and Silky's the only one here. And you said two children, and there are three of us – Milo, Mia and I'm Birdy,' she said.

'It's just to fit my song. I always have to begin with two. It sounds better. Pleased to meet you, Birdy and Mia and Milo. And lovely to see you too, dear Silky. This is my friend Mr Watzisname – and I am the Saucepan Man,' he added unnecessarily.

'I don't mean to be rude, but *why* have you got saucepans strung all over you?' Mia asked.

'Because I am the Saucepan Man,' he said.

Mr Watzisname stopped mid-snore. 'He used to sell them, but nowadays most folk buy them in stores or online,' he explained.

'So I've branched out into busking,' said the Saucepan Man. 'I'm quite well known in these parts for my drumming.'

'On saucepans?' said Milo.

'Well, we play kettledrums at school, don't we?' said Mia. 'Can you give us another song, Mr Saucepan Man?'

'Two horses here speeding,
Two horns gleaming white,
Two horses now feeding,
Oh, what a sight!'

he rapped to his own saucepan rhythm.

'Two horses are here?' said Mia. 'How can you have horses up a tree?'

'Not here, silly! Up there!' said the Saucepan Man, pointing upwards.

Silky gave a cry of joy. 'Oh, Saucepan, is the Land of Unicorns here?' she said.

'It is indeed,' said the Saucepan Man, grinning.

'The Land of *Unicorns?*' said all three children together.

'Come with me and I will show you!' said Silky.

CHAPTER SIX

THE CHILDREN followed Silky right to the very top of the Faraway Tree, talking excitedly.

'How can there possibly be another land at the *top* of the tree?' said Milo.

'And *unicorns*? They're not real,' said Mia.

Birdy stared at her brother and sister in astonishment. 'This is a *magic* tree!' she reminded them.

'That's right, Birdy, you tell them,' said Silky. 'They'll be saying fairies aren't real next!'

Milo and Mia laughed a little foolishly. They craned their necks – and saw a yellow ladder leading upwards into a dense white cloud.

'We climb up the ladder?' said Milo.

'That's right,' said Silky.

'And that's unicorn land up there?' said Mia.

They were still wondering whether this could be Silky's tease, as it still didn't seem possible, magic or not. But then they heard a strange pounding above, distant but distinct.

'It sounds like horses!' said Mia. Mum and Dad said they couldn't afford riding lessons for her, but she'd often watched children on their ponies cantering in the big park. 'Two horses speeding, like the Saucepan Man said in his song. Only this sounds like lots of horses!'

'With horns gleaming white!' said Milo.

'*Unicorns!*' said Birdy, starting to climb the ladder after Silky.

'Hang on, Birdy. I'd better go first,' said Milo. 'And you go behind to help her, Mia.'

'I don't need help!' said Birdy, and hurried so determinedly that her foot slipped sideways and she very nearly put her leg through the rung of the ladder. But she saved herself in time and climbed up until her head and shoulders and arms disappeared into the cloud.

'Are you all right, Birdy?' Milo called anxiously.

They heard her give a squeal of joy, though it was muffled by the cloud.

'Sounds like she's seeing unicorns!' said Mia. 'Come on!'

They climbed the ladder too. Milo disappeared into the cloud, and then Mia rushed after him. The cloud was very soft and billowy, not damp like a rain cloud. It felt so pleasant they might have stayed to enjoy it properly, but they couldn't wait to see the unicorns. Then their heads burst clear of the cloud, first Milo, then Mia, and they scrambled clear to stand beside Birdy and Silky in the Land of Unicorns.

The sky seemed much bluer up above the cloud, and the sun shone so brightly they blinked, getting used to it. They were standing in a beautiful meadow, the green grass covered in cowslips and ox-eye daisies and pink wild orchids. There were little glades and a small foxglove wood. More fields stretched beyond, with deep-blue and purple hills in the far distance. And there were the unicorns, nibbling grass in the meadow, lying peacefully, galloping swiftly across the fields – and one all alone, far away at the top of the tallest hill, turned into a small silhouette.

The unicorns shone in the sunlight, utterly dazzling. They weren't like the unicorns the children had seen in fairy-tale books. They weren't simply horses with horns. They were a totally different species, leaner and more elegant than any horse, yet clearly powerful and muscular. Some were pearly white, some were silvery grey, some were a rich yellow like gold, some were a warm bronze brown, some a shiny jet black – and each had a single ivory horn in the middle of its forehead. Their heads were beautiful, their eyes large and thickly lashed. Their manes flowed past their shoulders, and their tails were great plumes almost down to the ground.

Milo and Mia and Birdy all held hands, standing utterly still, scarcely daring to blink. But Silky ran

THE MAGIC FARAWAY TREE

forward eagerly, her arms outstretched – and one of the unicorns spotted her and came cantering swiftly towards her. His horn gleamed at every twist, its pointed end sharper than any knife.

'Be careful, Silky!' the children called – but there was no need.

The unicorn stopped at her side, his horn lowered to the ground. Silky flung her arms round his beautiful arched neck and rubbed her cheek against his smooth head. She wasn't quite tall enough to do this comfortably, so she unfurled her wings and let them lift her ten centimetres above the ground, her feet dangling.

'Darling Stardust, I've missed you so!' she cried, nestling into him so that her long golden hair mingled with his silvery mane.

He made a strange, soft whistling sound, a little like a horse's neigh, but much more melodic. It made no sense to the children at first, but they found if they concentrated very hard, they could understand some of what he said. He had missed Silky too and was delighted when his land came to rest at the top of the Faraway Tree. He asked who her three companions were.

Silky beckoned to the children and they approached hesitantly.

'This is my special friend Birdy – and her brother and sister, Milo and Mia,' said Silky.

Birdy glowed with pride at being called special. She ran right up to Stardust and smiled at him.

'Yes, I'm Birdy, and I'm very pleased to meet you, Stardust,' she said.

He gently pawed the ground in greeting, and whistled, saying something about being pleased to meet her too.

'Come on Mia, Milo. There's no need to be afraid,' said Birdy, which annoyed them.

'I'm not one bit afraid,' said Mia, and she reached out and stroked Stardust's neck.

'I'm not either,' said Milo, and patted Stardust on his back, barely touching him.

'Is Stardust your very own unicorn, Silky?' Birdy asked.

'You can't own a unicorn. They are spirited

magical creatures who own themselves,' Silky told her gently. 'But Stardust is my special friend. I've known you since you were a little foal, haven't I?' she said, running her fingers through Stardust's magnificent mane.

He whistled something else. Birdy was the first to understand.

'He says he's got his own foal now!' she cried. 'Oh, can we see it, please!'

Stardust nodded proudly and trotted towards a small glade of trees. There was another adult unicorn there, a bit smaller, with an even longer mane and tail. She looked warily at the children, but Stardust blew through his nostrils, reassuring her. She moved to one side, and behind her there was a little foal lying on the grass, sleeping. His horn was still very small, though already intricately twisted with a tiny point at the end.

Stardust told Silky that his mate was called Silver and she had chosen the name Little Star for their son. Silver nodded her head and whinnied a greeting, and Little Star opened his eyes at the sound of his name. He blinked sleepily.

'Oh, isn't he *lovely*!' Birdy said. 'Can I stroke him?'

'No, you mustn't,' said Mia, hanging on to Birdy's arm. She knew you should never stroke baby animals because their mother might think you were harming them.

But Silky knelt down beside Silver and Little Star, nodded her head respectfully to the mother and then stroked the foal. Fairies didn't seem to know the rules. When Little Star responded happily, nuzzling against her, she blew into his tiny nostrils and tickled him under his chin, so that he kicked his wobbly legs in delight.

'*I* want to play with him too!' said Birdy, pulling free from Mia.

'Of course, as long as Silver doesn't mind,' said Silky, but she was careful to put her hand over Birdy's and guide it.

Mia couldn't help feeling irritated, because she badly wanted to stroke the foal too. Milo was stroking Stardust now, a little cautiously at first, but the unicorn stood still placidly. Milo felt in his shorts pocket and found a Polo mint. Mia had told him once that horses liked peppermints, so he put it on the palm of his hand and offered it to him. Stardust sniffed it and then gently opened his mouth and took the Polo. He crunched it eagerly.

'Do you have another Polo?' Mia asked Milo. 'Could I feed him too?'

'Sorry, that was my last one,' said Milo.

'We'll find you lots more unicorns to feed, Mia,' said Silky, giving Little Star one last stroke. 'They're all very friendly, apart from the sea unicorns, but they live far away, over the mountains. We'll leave Silver and Little Star in peace.'

Stardust stayed with his family while Silky and the children walked across the meadow, pausing to say hello to every unicorn they came across. Some half-grown unicorns were galloping up and down, heads thrust forward, manes and tails flying. An adult unicorn was watching, tapping his hooves. They were discoloured and his coat was patchy, showing his great age, but he had a true dignity about him, and his eyes were still sharp and all-seeing.

The half-grown unicorns all seemed very eager to please him.

'They're racing each other!' said Milo. 'And the big unicorn's like their PE teacher! I race too, Silky. Actually, I sometimes win.' He *always* won, but he didn't want to sound too boastful.

'We used to have flying races when I was at Enchanter School,' said Silky. 'I sometimes won too.'

'I often win as well,' said Mia, though she felt foolish echoing the others.

'They will have a short break in a minute,' said Silky. 'Shall we pick some fruit from the trees, so they can have a little snack?'

The branches were covered with clusters of strange fruit like giant pink and purple strawberries.

'Oh, yum!' said Birdy, picking a snack for herself. 'I crayoned the unicorns pink and purple in my colouring book at home. And I put ribbons on their manes and tails. Do you think I could do that with these unicorns?'

'I think they like their manes and tails to blow freely in the wind, but you could try,' said Silky.

'Only not the sea unicorns! They're much too wild and spirited.'

Mia narrowed her eyes and peered at the horizon. The silhouette at the top of the mountain had moved a bit nearer. It was impossible to tell properly at this distance, but from the way his head was angled he seemed to be looking at her. She felt her heart thumping. She started walking in his direction, almost as if she was in a dream, but Milo ran after her, tugging at her arm.

'Where are you going?' he asked.

Mia nodded towards the unicorn. He was coming down the mountain now, his long horn glinting in the sunlight. It was hard to make out what colour he was. Sometimes he shone green, sometimes turquoise, sometimes midnight blue.

'You're not going anywhere near him!' said Milo. 'He must be one of the sea unicorns. Look, the young ones have finished their race. Let's see who won.'

He pulled Mia back with him, though she kept turning her head, wanting to see if the wild unicorn was getting nearer. The young ones were all trotting up and down, breathing a little heavily. The teacher singled one out and touched his shoulder with his horn, while all the others whistled.

'He must be the winner! Well done!' said Milo. He picked a giant strawberry and offered it to the proud young unicorn.

'My teacher says we're *all* winners when we race,' said Birdy. 'So you lot are all winners too. I'm going to feed you loads of this funny fruit.'

They gathered round Birdy, pressing their heads against her, snuffling hungrily. She giggled and gave them a berry each. They weren't all as dainty as Stardust.

'I've got lick all over me!' said Birdy, but she didn't mind.

The old unicorn was in earnest conversation with Silky. She clapped her hands excitedly.

'Guess what! The tutor here is suggesting this would be a good opportunity for his oldest pupils to learn the skill of carrying,' Silky said.

'Carrying?' said Mia, forgetting about the sea

unicorn now. 'You mean carrying *us*? So we're *riding* them?'

'Yes, if you'd like that,' said Silky.

'If we'd *like* it?' said Mia. 'We would absolutely love it!'

The young unicorns seemed enthusiastic too. The one who had won the race came right up to Milo and nuzzled in his hand, perhaps still smelling the Polo mint.

'I want to ride on this one!' said Milo. 'What's your name, clever unicorn?'

The young ones couldn't manage to speak their language the way Stardust could, but it didn't seem to matter.

'I shall call you Winner!' Milo declared. 'Can I get on your back?'

He'd only ever ridden a donkey at the seaside. That was a very different docile creature, who'd had a saddle and bridle and a stirrup to put a foot in. This was a lively prancing unicorn unused to anyone at all on his back, but he was willing all the same. Milo stuck his leg up and tried very hard to scramble on to his back. He had to make three attempts, looking very clumsy, but eventually managed to haul himself into place. Winner whinnied, sounding as if he was laughing at him.

'I don't think I'm big enough to do that!' said Birdy.

Silky led the smallest unicorn to her. It was little older than the foal, but very sturdy on its legs, and rather chubby, like a Shetland pony.

'Oh! This one's so sweet!' Birdy breathed. 'Can I call you Sweetie?'

'You can't call a unicorn Sweetie!' said Milo, wrinkling his nose.

'Yes I can!' said Birdy. 'Look, she likes her name!'

Sweetie looked very happy, especially when Birdy gave her one last strawberry. Mia picked Birdy up and managed to get her into place on Sweetie's back with one swift heave.

'That's it! Sit up as straight as you can. Hold on to her mane, but gently. Try to bob up and down with her when she moves,' said Mia.

She looked round, trying to decide which unicorn

she should ride. She chose another female with a fine spirited air about her.

'Perhaps I could call you Spirit?' Mia asked.

Spirit nodded in approval.

'Shall I help you on to her back?' Silky offered.

'I think I can manage myself,' said Mia, praying that she was right. She knew exactly how to do it inside her head, but she had no more actual experience of riding than Milo. She took a deep breath, ran a little, put one hand on Spirit's firm back and vaulted into place.

'Well done!' said Silky, and the tutor himself neighed congratulations.

Mia patted Spirit gratefully and sat up proudly. Even Milo was impressed.

'How did you know how to do that?' he asked.

Mia shrugged. 'I just did,' she said casually, as if it were no big deal. She was hugging herself inside.

Stardust came cantering over to see how they were doing. The tutor had a word with him in their own language. Stardust bowed his head at Silky, and she jumped right up on to his back. It was a much bigger leap for her, but she did it as gracefully as Mia, though she did flap her wings a little.

The tutor gathered the rest of the young unicorns into a tidy line, their horns all sticking up at the same angle, and told them to pay attention. Then Silky trotted up and down on Stardust, her head up, her back straight. Stardust moved with ease and grace, as if he had a butterfly on his back. All the young unicorns neighed their approval.

Then it was Milo's turn. He could feel himself going bright red as they all stared at him with their intense blue eyes. Winner seemed agitated too, shifting from hoof to hoof and turning his head.

'We can do it, Winner!' Milo whispered into his ear. 'We're winners!'

Winner started walking slowly forward, giving Milo time to get used to the strange rhythm. He mastered it almost straight away, though he had to grip tight with his knees to stop himself slipping off Winner's smooth back. Then they tried cantering, which was much more difficult. Milo had to grab hold of Winner's mane and cling hard – but they managed it and received their neigh of approval.

'Can Sweetie and I go next? I always have to come last just because I'm the youngest,' said Birdy.

Silky stood beside her and led her along just in case she fell. Sweetie was small but she had a very round back and a rather stompy gait, so Birdy bounced all over the place, but Silky always managed to catch her before she slid right off. The young unicorns snickered a little, because they did look rather comical, but gave them a neigh of approval too.

'Our turn now, Spirit!' Mia whispered. She nudged her heels against Spirit's sides and they started trotting. They moved so smoothly it was as if they were one magical creature – half girl, half unicorn. Mia urged Spirit into a canter, and then couldn't help showing off and attempting a really fast gallop. Spirit wasn't so sure now. She was only young and not used to moving so quickly with a girl on her back. Mia sensed her hesitancy and immediately urged her to slow down, not wanting her to stumble. They slowed and then stopped a bit abruptly. An uncertain rider like Birdy might well have fallen off then, but Mia stayed firmly seated, smiling.

It had still been a majestic performance and the young unicorns neighed with great enthusiasm. The tutor nodded congratulations too, but said something that sounded a little reproving. Mia guessed that he felt Spirit was too young to be attempting a gallop.

Spirit was somewhat subdued, but Mia felt indignant. She wanted to go really, really fast. She stroked Spirit to console her and then looked up to meet a pair of midnight-blue eyes. The sea unicorn was standing near the young unicorns. They spotted him and bowed their heads a little fearfully. Even the tutor shuffled respectfully. The sea unicorn was several hands higher than any other full-grown unicorn. His horn was longer than any spear and shone like polished silver. He stood still, tall and magnificent, lean but muscular, the most beautiful and powerful animal Mia had ever seen.

Mia could feel Spirit trembling beneath her. She

patted the young unicorn gratefully and then slid off her back. She walked slowly, cautiously, towards the huge unicorn.

'No, Mia!' said Silky. 'He's too strong, too wild! Don't go near him!'

The tutor said something sharply too. Milo tried to get hold of her again, but she pushed him away. Birdy begged her, but Mia barely noticed them. It was as if she was under a spell. She walked until she was standing right in front of the wild unicorn, staring up at him. She reached up and stroked his great head with a trembling hand.

'Do you ever let anyone ride on your back?' she whispered.

He didn't try to answer in any kind of speech, but he lowered his head as if he were saying he might.

'He's far too big for you!' Silky cried. 'You can't ride him! It's much too dangerous! He might carry you over the mountains and right out to sea.'

Mia couldn't help herself. The sea unicorn was twice the size of Spirit, and it had taken all her strength to jump on to her back, but she tried to mount the sea unicorn all the same. She took a deep breath and leapt upwards and somehow managed to land on the sea unicorn's sleek back. He waited a second for her to steady herself and started galloping.

Mia had to thrust her fingers deep into his long silky mane to stay on. She couldn't steer him in any way. She certainly couldn't stop him. She just had to grip as hard as she could and stay perched high up on his back.

There was a great cry behind her. She turned her head with difficulty and saw Silky trying to gallop after her on Stardust, with Milo valiantly behind her on Winner, even though they didn't have a hope of catching up with her.

'Don't worry! I'm fine!' she shouted into the wind, nearly slipping. She didn't dare look back after that. She *was* fine. She was more than fine. She was so thrilled she wanted to scream and sing, but she didn't have any more breath. She'd never been so happy, so scared, so wonderfully alive.

They hurtled forward, across the meadow, jumping the hedge in a perfect arc, over the fields, on and on towards the faraway mountains. There were unicorns feeding, trotting, drinking from a stream, all pausing and staring in wonder at the huge sea unicorn with the small girl on his broad back.

Mia risked freeing one hand to wave to them, getting more confident now. Her eyes watered in the wind and she was starting to ache with the effort of staying on his back, but she still didn't ever want him to stop. They were near the mountains now, greener as they got nearer, and covered with fruit bushes – multicoloured currants and gooseberries as well as the giant strawberries. She saw several other unicorns grazing, all beautiful, but her own sea unicorn was by far the biggest and the best.

He didn't slow his stride even though the slope was steep. He galloped up and up and up until at last they were on the narrow summit, high above the whole land. He stopped then, scarcely out of breath, arching his neck proudly. Mia gazed all round her in awe. She could see plains and prairies and then white cliffs and a long stretch of golden sand and deep-blue sea the other side of the mountain.

'It's so beautiful,' Mia gasped.

He nodded towards the sea as if in enquiry.

'Do I want to go on?' Mia said.

She knew she'd been gone a very long time already, but time didn't count here, did it? She also knew that Milo and Birdy and Silky would be worried about her, and she should turn back for their sakes. But the sea glittered magically in the distance and she couldn't help herself.

'Oh, please, yes! Let's go all the way to the sea!' she cried.

So they travelled down, down, down the mountain, across the plains and the prairies, all the way to the white cliffs, and then the sea unicorn had to slow at last because there was only a steep, narrow pathway cut in the chalk to the beach far below. He didn't falter once, his gleaming hooves picking their way steadily downwards until at last they were on the golden sand.

The air was fresh and salty here, and they could both feel the refreshing cool of the sea spray. Mia slid down off the unicorn's back to let him have a rest at last. They wandered across the warm sand to the water's edge and then looked at each other.

'Yes, let's!' said Mia.

She rolled up her jeans and let the water lap at her toes, washing the sand away. The unicorn stepped daintily through the waves, amusing himself by dancing in an intricate pattern, but then he faced out to sea, arching his neck. He started swimming, very slowly at first so that Mia could keep up with

him. Then he let her come really close and slide on to his back, clutching his long mane so that she wouldn't be swept away. He swam through the deep-blue sea until Mia wondered if they might be swimming to the horizon and beyond and she suddenly panicked. 'Not too far,' she cried. The unicorn swung his head, looking at her. He breathed out heavily through his nostrils, treading water so he could consider. Then he turned, watching the waves, and suddenly leapt up so that they could surf all the way back to the shore.

They landed in the shallows and Mia leant forward and hugged him gratefully. She blinked in the strong sunlight, seeing dazzling spray-drops on her wet eyelashes. She rubbed her eyes, trying to focus. There was a white unicorn scarcely visible against the chalk cliff, carrying someone with long hair as gold as the sand.

'Silky!' said Mia.

Stardust trotted over the sand and the sea unicorn waded out of the sea. Stardust lowered his horn in deference. The sea unicorn stood proudly.

'Oh, Mia! Are you all right?' Silky said anxiously.

'It's time you came back!'

'I don't want to!' said Mia. 'And time doesn't mean anything up in this land. I could stay here for days and days and then go home and no one would have missed me.'

'Milo and Birdy are missing you now,' said Silky. 'It's too far for them to come and fetch you. Milo's so worried – and Birdy can't stop crying.'

Mia wanted to put her hands over her ears. She didn't want to hear about Milo and Birdy. She didn't want to feel guilty. She just wanted to stay with the sea unicorn and speed around this magical land for ever.

But she loved her brother and sister. She couldn't help imagining Milo's face, grey and pinched, with sharp frown lines above his nose. She thought of Birdy with tears dripping down her cheeks, calling for her.

Mia sighed long and hard. She bent her head, burying her face in the unicorn's silky mane. She breathed in his strange salty smell and stroked his smooth head.

'I think I have to go back now,' she whispered to him.

He understood, but rubbed his great head against hers sadly. He carried her all the way back over the mountain, going more slowly now, both of them weighed down with sadness. He stopped at the edge of the bright meadow, and Mia slid reluctantly down from his back.

'I will come back tomorrow,' she promised. 'And the next day and the next day and the next.'

She liked to say that she never ever cried, but her eyes watered as she stood watching him go.

CHAPTER SEVEN

THE CHILDREN were exhausted by the time they trailed home – but Mum and Dad were still drinking coffee, the breakfast dishes on the table.

'Hello, you three!' said Dad. 'You haven't been gone long!

'You haven't had an argument, have you?' said Mum, looking at them carefully. Somehow they had to pretend that they'd simply been playing in the lane.

Even Birdy managed not to say anything about unicorns, but she was very clingy that day, and hung on to Mia's hand a lot of the time. Milo hardly said a word to Mia, still angry that she had gone off with the sea unicorn – and perhaps a bit envious that she'd had such an adventure.

Mia was still imagining herself on the wild unicorn's back, riding far away in that distant magical land. She ached all over from the long ride, but she pressed her lips together, determined not to complain. She barely said a word. She knew Milo was very cross with her and Birdy was still hiccupping a little after crying, but she wasn't ready to say sorry. She was just trying to work out a way to get back to the Faraway Tree on her own.

However, Mum and Dad took them for a special day out to a children's petting zoo, and it was impossible not to enjoy stroking the rabbits and guinea pigs and scratching the pigs on their backs. They queued for a donkey ride too. They were lovely donkeys, with big ears and warm brown eyes, but they seemed very ordinary compared to unicorns. It was all so different from the thrills of the Faraway Tree.

By the time they got home they were so tired they could barely stay awake for supper. In fact Birdy fell asleep at the table, resting her head on her arms, and Milo kept yawning loudly.

'You're all such sleepyheads today,' said Dad.

'It must be the fresh country air,' said Mum.

'*I'm* not sleepy,' Mia insisted, though she had huge dark circles under her eyes. 'I feel so restless and fidgety. Maybe I need to have a little walk. It's OK – I'll go by myself.'

'Oh no you won't!' said Milo, guessing what she was plotting. 'She's not allowed to go out by herself, is she?'

'Of course not!' said Mum. 'Come on upstairs, all of you. Have a nice bath, Mia – that will stop you feeling fidgety.'

The hot bath was certainly soothing, and helped ease Mia's sore muscles, but her head still reeled thinking about the wild unicorn. She didn't think she'd sleep a wink that night, but in fact she fell asleep in the middle of Milo giving her a lecture.

Birdy struggled to stay awake to wave to Silky, but it was impossible. She fell fast asleep clutching Gilbert, though he felt very stiff and matted after

Sweetie's warm skin and silky mane.

They all overslept the next morning, even Mia. When she woke up she went and sat on the edge of Milo's bed. He was hunched up under the covers, just his hair sticking out.

'Hey, Milo,' Mia said softly. She twirled a lock of his hair round her finger and pulled very gently. 'Sorry I went off yesterday and got you in such a state.'

'Stop messing with my hair,' said Milo, surfacing. 'I wasn't in a *state*, I was just worried about you being so stupid. Even Silky was going mad, and the tutor and all the other unicorns. Nobody ever tries to ride a wild unicorn!'

'Well, I did,' said Mia proudly. 'And I'm going to again. I'm going back today. I have to see him. I promised I'd come back.'

'Oh, Mia!' said Milo. 'OK, you were fine yesterday, and you're brilliant at riding, but it's a wild animal, and Silky says you never know when they'll suddenly turn on you. You wouldn't try to ride a *tiger*, would you?'

'Yes I would,' said Mia. She was teasing, but Milo took her seriously.

'Look, I'm going to have to tell Mum and Dad if you keep on like this,' he said.

'Oh, yeah, and what are you going to tell them, eh? Naughty Mia goes riding on a wild unicorn up over the mountains and down to the sea?' said Mia. 'As if they'd believe you!'

'I'm only going on like this because I care about you, you fool,' said Milo, pushing her and catching her off balance, so she nearly toppled off the bed.

'Don't you push me!' she said, giving him a shove back.

They ended up wrestling, and then tickling each other, laughing hysterically. They woke Birdy upstairs and she came hurrying down the ladder.

'Are we fighting? Can I join in too?' she asked excitedly.

'You know it's not a proper fight, Birdy. We're friends really,' said Mia. She looked at Milo. 'I won't go as far on my unicorn next time, I promise. I won't even ride him if you really insist. But I must go back, because I promised. Don't you want to see Stardust and Silver and their foal? And Winner?'

'I want to see my Sweetie!' said Birdy.

So it was decided. As soon as Mum and Dad started on a fresh pot of coffee at breakfast, the children begged to go and play in the lane for a while.

'I don't know what's so exciting about that funny little lane,' said Mum.

'We have races,' Milo said quickly.

'Well, I can see that's fun for you, darling, because you always win,' said Mum.

'I win too,' said Mia.

'And I do too,' Birdy insisted, though that was obviously not true.

'Tell you what, I'll take my coffee with me and come and supervise,' said Dad. 'Perhaps you could all have a skipping race, or a walking backwards race, or a hopping race? That would be fun, wouldn't it?'

The children were horrified – and yet they didn't want to hurt Dad's feelings.

'Maybe later, Dad,' Mia said. 'But we're fine by ourselves now, honestly.'

'Thanks though,' Milo added.

'I love you, Dad. And Mum,' Birdy gabbled, and then they all rushed out of the back door, down the garden and through the gate before Mum and Dad could say another word.

They ran to the start of the Enchanted Wood, just to be able to say they really had run a race. Milo won, though Mia was only a second behind. Birdy came puffing along third.

'When I'm grown-up I'm going to be able to beat both of you,' she said. She was peering across the ditch into the dark trees.

'I wonder if the rabbit will take us to the Faraway Tree this time. Or will it be the little fawn?' she said.

They all waited. It didn't look as if anyone was coming. They looked at each other, feeling a bit foolish.

'Perhaps we can find our own way,' said Milo, trying to sound convincing.

'After all, we've been there twice already,' said Mia.

'I could just call for Silky,' said Birdy. She cleared

her throat and then yelled, 'SILKY! SILKY! SILKY!'

Milo and Mia backed away from her, their hands over their ears. Birdy might have made little cheep sounds when she'd been a baby, but now she could bellow like a fire alarm. She made the rooks in the trees rise up, cawing at her indignantly. The children stared at them hopefully, wondering if they might show them the way, but after circling several times they returned to their nests with a flutter of wings.

Birdy still peered upwards, hoping to see Silky, but she didn't come. Neither did the rabbit nor the fawn. But then Mia clutched Birdy's hand and Milo's shoulder.

'Look!' she whispered.

A black bear was peering round a tree at them. Not a terrifying big bear. A very tiny bear, smaller than Birdy. He didn't look frightening. He was the one who looked frightened. He was actually sucking his paw for comfort.

'Hello, little bear!' Mia said very softly.

He blinked at her. Then he whispered, 'Hello!'

He said it in a mumble because he still had his paw
in his mouth, but it was clear he was actually talking.

'Oh, he's just a baby!' said Birdy.

'Are you all on your own, little bear?' Milo asked,
peering cautiously round in case a very big father or
mother bear were lurking.

'All on my own,' he said. 'I'm lost. I've been lost
for ages and ages, wandering in the woods. I was so
hungry I climbed a tree to see if I could find some
honey, but the bees all stung me, so I fell down. A
very kind fairy called Silky put some magic ointment
on my stings and gave me a lovely honey sandwich

and set me on my way to the dark woods where the bears live, but I got lost again. Do you know Silky? I heard you calling her.' He was so exhausted by his long speech that he sat down and started crying.

'Oh, you poor little thing!' said Mia, kneeling down beside him. She put her arm round him and he wriggled on to her lap and clung to her, more like a koala than a small black bear.

'I want to cuddle him too!' said Birdy, sitting down.

'What's your name, little bear?' Milo asked, squatting beside them.

The bear sniffed and wiped his eyes against Mia's T-shirt, though she didn't mind a bit. He opened and closed his mouth, thinking hard.

'I can't remember,' he said at last, and started crying again.

'Don't worry. I expect it's because you've been lost for so long. And we know a man called Mr Watzisname because he can't remember his name either, even though he's never got lost as far as I know. He lives at the Faraway Tree with Silky and lots of other interesting people. Let's see if we can find them,' said Milo.

He was a bit worried that they might *all* get lost, and indeed when they started walking into the wood it seemed likely. They blundered this way and that, trying so hard to remember the right path, but all the trees looked alike. *Wisha-wisha-wisha* they whispered, a little mockingly.

'Well, I *wisha-wisha-wisha* you'd show us the right way,' said Milo.

The wind suddenly started blowing, only really a light breeze, but somehow it was enough to rustle the trees and shake their branches. Their *wisha-wisha-wisha* grew louder, and Milo saw that the branches of the nearest tree seemed all to be pointing one way. He looked at the next tree, and the next.

'The trees themselves are showing us the way!' he said.

It was so easy to find their way right to the Faraway Tree. The trees pointed down one path and up the next, and every so often a rabbit or squirrel peeped out and pointed too. Even small mice and voles jumped up out of the grass, waving their tiny paws the right way.

'Are they food?' the little bear asked Mia hopefully.

'No, they're helpful friends!' said Mia. 'Don't worry – we'll find you something to eat as soon as we get to the Faraway Tree. I think we're nearly there.'

They were soon right in front of it, the biggest tree of all, as round as a tower. The children started climbing. Mia had to climb one-handed because she was still holding the little bear, but he soon gained confidence and started scrambling upwards himself. The tree was growing apples now, all different varieties on the same branch – rosy Pink Ladies, greeny-brown Russets, and red and yellow Cox's Orange Pippins.

'Are *these* food?' the little bear asked.

'Yes, you can pick as many as you like,' said Mia.

They sat on a big branch and had an apple feast, trying to decide which type they liked best. Birdy liked the Pink Lady sort, Milo preferred the Russets, and Mia and the little bear decided that

Cox's Orange Pippins were the best.

'Cox's Orange Pippin!' the little bear said, chuckling at the funny name. He had one in each paw and was munching both at once.

'You'll turn into a Cox's Orange Pippin if you carry on eating so many!' said Mia. 'Hey, shall we call you that? I think Cox's Orange Pippin is a splendid name.'

It was a bit long for such a small bear, so they settled on Pippin. He smiled happily every time they said his new name.

'I know a very magic place where you can get special giant berries,' said Mia. 'There are unicorns there! Would you like to go and see them?'

Pippin nodded, though he didn't have a clue what unicorns were. They started the long climb upwards, Pippin happily darting this way and that, helping himself to more apples, careful only to select Cox's Orange Pippins.

'Come here, Pippin, quick!' Mia warned as they approached the Angry Pixie's house, not wanting the little bear to be shouted at.

But strangely the pixie's window was shut and the children remained bone dry. They decided he must have gone out early. The children often glanced up warily, ready to dodge Dame Washalot's soapy water, but she didn't seem to be washing today. And when they got to Silky's lovely yellow door there was no answer when they knocked.

'Where's my Silky?' Birdy asked, upset.

'*My* Silky!' said Pippin. 'Who will look after me now?'

'I will,' said Mia, giving him a cuddle.

'It's so strange that everyone's out today,' said Milo.

'Maybe they've all gone for a ride down Moonface's slippery-slip,' Mia suggested. She was just a little bit relieved that Silky wasn't around. Silky had given her a rather uncomfortable scolding yesterday about the dangers of riding sea unicorns. Mia knew she'd meant it kindly, but it still made her squirm.

They went up the tree to see if Mia might be right. Pippin hung on to her now. As they got near

Moonface's house it was clear that he *was* at home – and he seemed to have many guests too. There was a great clamour of high-pitched chattering and they heard Moonface groaning in seeming despair.

'What on earth's happened?' said Milo. 'Stand back, girls, I'll go first.'

'*I* will! I'm the one with a savage bear!' said Mia. 'Growl, Pippin!' He gave a rather pathetic squeak.

Birdy was the one who darted through the open door first, while the others dithered. She found herself waist-deep in squirrels, all leaping about excitedly. The red squirrel who collected the cushions was standing in their midst, hands on his hips, his bushy tail thumping the floor furiously. Moonface and Silky were sitting at a table overflowing with old magic textbooks, frantically thumbing their way through the yellowed pages.

'Oh, Silky, what's happened?' said Birdy, running to her.

'Silky, Silky, Silky!' said Pippin, jumping down from Mia to rush to her.

'Careful, careful, my loves!' said Silky. She was

wearing a pretty purple dress, her wings tinged lavender, but the strong colour didn't seem to suit her because her face looked very pale.

'Watch where you're treading!' said Moonface. *His* face was so flushed he looked more a setting-sun-face, and he seemed on the brink of tears.

The children looked down where he was pointing. There was a pile of very tiny rubbish scattered on the carpet – miniature lemonade bottles, scraps of chocolate wrappers, weeny ice-cream cartons, little scribbled notes and newspapers and discarded clothing, check trousers, smart blazers, fancy scarves and embroidered slippers small enough to fit a finger-sized Moonface. There, jumping up and down excitedly on these minute remnants, was the smallest squirrel in the world.

'My eldest son, Tipkin!' cried the red squirrel dramatically. He shook his paw at Moonface. 'Turn him back to full size this instant!'

'I'm trying, I'm trying,' said Moonface, tears running down his round reddened cheeks. 'I just can't remember the magic words. They're on the tip of my tongue, I promise you. And they're written down in one of these books, but I just can't find the right page.'

'Moonface had another party with the squirrels last night. They all fell fast asleep and woke up to chaos in the morning,' Silky explained to the children.

'And I knew I was in for another telling-off from dear Silky,' said Moonface, thumbing through the pages of his magic books. 'But then I hit on a wonderful idea. One of the first things you learn in magic class is the shrinking spell. You're all given a watermelon and you say this magic spell that goes—'

'No! Don't say it again, whatever you do!' said Silky.

Moonface put his hand over his mouth, choking back the words. He swallowed hard.

'And the watermelon shrinks to the size of a grape! It's a very popular spell because you're allowed to eat it afterwards and it tastes divine. So anyway, I thought I'd reduce all our rubbish, so that it could be swept up in one swift go. I said the magic words—'

'Careful!' Silky warned.

'Though I wasn't very sure I remembered them, because I'm so out of practice. But I must have got them in the right order because when I pointed, lo and behold – the rubbish shrank!' said Moonface, waving at it miserably. 'But my discarded clothes shrank too, which was a pity, because I'm especially fond of that scarlet jacket and pair of checked trousers – and even more unfortunately, I was also inadvertently pointing in the direction of my special squirrel friend, Tipkin, who shrank at an alarming rate.'

'My eldest son reduced to a tiny toy!' the red squirrel thundered. 'Turn him back to normal size immediately, you moon-faced fool!'

'I'm trying, I'm trying,' said Moonface desperately.

'Don't be cross, Dad – I *like* being little!' Tipkin squeaked. 'It's fun! I shall always win when we play hide-and-seek.'

'Have some common sense, boy! You'll get trodden

on and squashed – or mistaken as a tasty snack by a wild animal,' said the red squirrel, glaring at Pippin.

'*Is* it a tasty snack?' Pippin whispered to Mia.

'Absolutely not!' said Mia quickly.

'You can have one of my honey cakes when we've found the increasing spell, little bear. But meanwhile I think you'd all better go, because we have to concentrate on finding the right spell, and Mr Red is right – poor Tipkin could easily get trodden on!' said Silky. 'I should pick him up if I were you.'

The red squirrel picked up his diminutive son and held him carefully in the palm of his paw.

'My poor boy!' he said and burst into a flood of tears.

'Hey, don't cry, Dad – you're getting me all wet!' said Tipkin, splashing up and down merrily.

The children very much wanted to stay, but could see they were making the room inconveniently overcrowded.

'We'll go up to the Land of Unicorns and pop back later,' said Mia, making her way back through the overexcited squirrels to the door, Pippin in her arms and Birdy and Milo following.

Silky was so distressed she didn't take in what Mia was saying at first. But then she shouted, 'No, Mia! Wait!'

Mia didn't want to wait for another lecture about the dangers of wild unicorns, so she pretended not to hear and shut the door. They climbed the tree and discovered most of the other folk were out somewhere. Dame Washalot's tub was empty, the washing neatly pegged to a line between two branches, but there was no sign of the dame herself. The Saucepan Man's and Mr Watzisname's deckchairs were in their usual places, but the two old gentlemen were missing.

'Perhaps they're all up in the Land of Unicorns,' said Milo.

'Well, it is lovely there,' said Mia. 'But I can't imagine any of them riding, can you?'

'I hope that the Saucepan Man doesn't try to get on to my Sweetie!' said Birdy. 'She'd hate all those saucepans clanking together.'

'Please could you tell me what unicorns *are*,' Pippin asked.

'They're the most beautiful magical creatures, a little like horses, and they've got one fantastic long horn sticking out of their foreheads. You will love them, Pippin,' said Mia.

Pippin wasn't so sure. He clutched Mia tightly and hid his head as she climbed up the ladder into the dense white cloud.

'Don't be frightened! Look!' said Mia, as she made her way through the cloud to the land above. And then she gasped in horror.

CHAPTER EIGHT

THERE WERE no unicorns, not even the smallest foal. There were no meadows, no flowers, no streams, no blue mountains, no sea unicorn watching for her. It was as if they had all been razed to the ground. In their place was a bizarre city of bouncy castles, in lurid pinks and blues and acid yellow.

All kinds of strange people and animals were bouncing frantically up and down, screaming their heads off: pixies, gnomes, goblins, rabbits, squirrels, even a herd of deer. Fairies flocked together, bouncing up to the sky and back, their wings outstretched. There were giants three times the size of the children, gambolling clumsily on the biggest castle, scissoring their tree-trunk legs at every bounce. Hedgehogs curled up into balls flew up and down in the air as if thrown by a six-armed juggler. Mice and voles and other scampering creatures bounced up and down in unison on one small castle and beetles and ladybirds and caterpillars bounced with their many tiny legs on the tiniest castle of all.

'Wow!' said Milo. He'd always adored bouncy castles at fairs and fetes and birthday parties. He jumped up the bouncy steps of the nearest castle and started leaping about, flinging his arms in the air.

'Let me have a go!' cried Birdy and ran up after him. It was a bigger bouncier castle than she was used to, so she found it hard to keep her footing at first, but she simply bounced on her bottom instead, laughing uproariously.

But Mia was near tears, peering round wildly.

'Where's the Land of Unicorns gone? What's happened?' she cried aloud.

Two cheeky goblins barged past her.

'Keep up! That was yesterday. It's the Land of

Bouncy Castles today, yay!' one said.

'You mean different lands come to the Faraway Tree every day?' Mia asked.

'Of course they do, silly! Don't you know anything?' said the other goblin rudely.

'But when will the Land of Unicorns come back?' Mia asked.

'This year, next year, sometime, never!' said the goblin, and leapt up after his companion.

They both bounced crazily, sticking their tongues out at poor Mia. She was still so upset she couldn't even be bothered to pull a face back. She sat down heavily on the trampled grass in front of the castle, despairing. Pippin clutched on to her, wondering if there might be any other bears in this strange bouncy land, but Mia wasn't paying him any attention. She could only think of her wild unicorn standing on top of the mountain, looking out for her, wondering why she wasn't coming as she'd promised.

An old lady in a mop cap and a long dress with a shawl round her large shoulders paused by Mia's side.

'Are you all right, little girl? Have you taken a

nasty tumble on one of the castles?' she asked.

'No, I haven't hurt myself. I'm just wishing my unicorn were here,' Mia said miserably.

'Oh, they wouldn't let any unicorns into the Land of Bouncy Castles, dearie! Think of those long, sharp horns. The castles would go off pop in a trice! Now *I'm* looking for an old friend of mine, Dame Washalot. She loves a good bounce. We used to come here when we were small girls at Laundry School. Have you seen her?' she said.

'Well, she wasn't at home in the Faraway Tree,' Mia said, looking round at all the bouncers. Then she suddenly spotted a similar old lady with a mop cap. She was on a nearby castle, leaping up and down in a comical manner, her long skirts hitched up, showing her big knickers. 'There she is!' she said, pointing.

'So she is. Dear Wilma! Yoo-hoo! It's me, my dear, Iris Ironallday!' She rushed off happily.

'Wilma Washalot and Iris Ironallday,' Mia muttered to herself, and she couldn't help giggling although she still felt miserable.

She watched Dame Ironallday climb up on to the next castle and bounce across to Dame Washalot. The friends embraced in delight, bouncing up and down in unison, cavorting around as if they really were schoolgirls again.

'Mia, watch me!' said Birdy, running about and falling down and running again, as if she were performing the most amazing acrobatic trick in the world.

'Mia, do come and have a go. It's absolutely great!' Milo called, attempting a somersault and nearly managing it.

Mia looked at Pippin. 'Do you want to have a go?' she asked him.

'Will it hurt a lot? I don't like falling over,' he said.

'If you fall, you'll simply bounce back. It doesn't hurt a bit. Look at Birdy,' she said.

'She's screaming!' said Pippin.

'That's because she's having fun,' said Mia.

Pippin didn't look at all convinced, but she stepped up on to the nearest castle while he was still clutching on to her. She bounced very gently. Pippin looked surprised. She bounced again, this way and that. Pippin started to smile. She bounced more, up to Birdy.

'Bounce with me, Pippin!' said Birdy, holding out both her hands.

Pippin jumped down and then found himself jumping up. And down. And up again. He started

laughing. Birdy grabbed his paws and they did a wild dance together. Mia bounced over to Milo, and they did a high five. Then Milo tried another somersault and perfected it this time. Mia had a go too. She landed on her head, but it didn't hurt a bit. She tried again, taking a giant leap, and this time tucked herself neatly into a ball, spinning round so that she landed neatly on her feet.

'Yay!' she shouted, holding out her arms, and Milo applauded her.

She still wished she were in the Land of Unicorns and ached to see the wild unicorn again – but she had to admit the Land of Bouncy Castles was great fun. They tried out all the castles. One was firmer, so that you could run round and round without falling over. Milo particularly liked this one because he could run faster than anyone else. Another was much bouncier, so that you shot right up in the air with time to turn several somersaults before you landed again. Mia loved showing off on this one, though a little group of wallabies were even better at bouncing and leapt even higher in a lively ring around her.

Birdy and Pippin liked the vast refreshment castle most of all. There were small hidey-holes all round the walls of this bouncy castle and you stuck a hand or paw in each one to get a treat – an apple, a sandwich, a carton of juice, a triangle of pizza, a fried chicken leg, a bag of crisps and many different cakes. Birdy bounced low and bounced high, helping herself to a large variety of snacks. Pippin found a special store of bread and honey and became very sticky indeed.

Milo and Mia came to join them and helped themselves too. It seemed like it was a general meeting place. The two laundry dames popped in for a cup of tea out of special sippy cups so that it didn't spill. The Angry Pixie was there, chewing on a chicken leg as he bounced. The children didn't recognise him at first because he was actually grinning, not the slightest bit angry.

They heard the Saucepan Man before they actually spotted him at the other end of the refreshment castle, his pots and pans clanging together like a noisy band as he bounced. Mr Watzisname was with him, doing wild jumping jacks in the air, a slice of pizza in each hand. He waved them at the children, and the Saucepan Man took off his saucepan hat and doffed it to them. Then they did a funny dance, twirling round and bumping their bottoms.

'Two dames who like jumping,
Two kids and their chum,
Two men who like bumping,
Bumpety, bumpety bum!'

the Saucepan Man sang, and they both doubled up laughing.

'Oh, Saucepan, you are funny,' said Milo, who loved silly jokes.

'But you still can't count,' said Birdy. 'We're *three* kids and their chum.'

'Am I the chum?' Pippin asked Mia hopefully.

'Of course you are. A very special one,' said Mia, picking him up and then rather regretting it because Pippin was incredibly sticky now.

Luckily Dame Washalot had a damp flannel in her pocket and Mia could wipe herself and Pippin too, though he protested.

'I really like tasting of honey!' he said, struggling to get away from her. Then he pointed at the entrance. 'Look, it's my Silky and the Moonface man!'

'*My* Silky!' said Birdy, as they all steadied

themselves and stared.

Silky was skipping up the steps to the refreshment castle, with Moonface staggering beside her, mopping his brow, beaming. Behind them came the red squirrel with a proper sized Tipkin – in fact he was a bit taller if anything, reaching right up to his father's shoulders now, and looking very proud of the fact. A merry bunch of overexcited little squirrels clustered after them, waving their tails like bushy flags.

'You remembered the spell to make him bigger!' said Milo, as Moonface bounced over to them, puffing out his chest and doing small sideways kicks.

'I rattled it off and, lo and behold, Tipkin grew! He's very pleased too. He'll be a legend in the squirrel community by tomorrow – and so shall I!' said Moonface. 'My goodness, making magic is hungry work!' He bounced up and grabbed a very large slice of chocolate cake from a cubby hole and started eating it with gusto.

'So did the words just come back to him?' Mia

asked Silky.

'He had a little reminder,' said Silky, smiling wryly. 'I managed to find the right spell written down in *Enchantments, Volume Two*.'

'Oh, Silky, you are clever!' said Birdy.

'Very, very clever,' said Pippin. 'Silky, do you think the spell would make *me* a bit bigger?'

'I think you're exactly the right size,' said Silky. 'If you turned into a great big bear, we'd all be frightened of you.'

'Would I really be scary?' asked Pippin, his eyes gleaming at the thought. 'Well, I'd never growl at *you*, Silky.'

'Even so, I think we've had enough magic for one day,' said Silky firmly. 'Oh my goodness, look! It's my clock! It must have climbed the tree and followed me all the way up the ladder!'

Silky's clock bounced over to them on its spidery little legs. It bounced higher and higher, growing so excited that it started chiming.

'One, two, three, four, five, six, seven, eight, nine, ten, eleven, twelve, *thirteen* . . . Hang on, clocks don't strike thirteen!' said Birdy, giggling.

'Silly clock! If you must strike, could you do it a bit more quietly?' Silky asked, patting him on his shiny wooden head.

Then she came over to Mia and put an arm round her.

'I'm so sorry the Land of Unicorns has moved on,' she said softly. 'I tried to tell you, but you went in too much of a hurry.'

'I know,' said Mia. She sighed. 'Won't it ever come back?'

'It will at some time. But we never know when because we don't really *have* time here. Look at my clock – it just chimes when it feels like it. But I promise I'll come and find you if the Land of Unicorns ever comes back while you're staying at the cottage – so long as you promise not to ride your wild unicorn so far that *you* never come back!' said Silky.

'Promise,' said Mia. 'But maybe I'll ride him *quite* far. Silky, what other lands come to the top of the Faraway Tree?

'There are too many to count. Some are wonderful,

some are simply strange, some are great fun – but some are very dangerous. We never know what's coming next,' said Silky. 'It's sometimes a brand-new land that surprises all of us.'

'Well, I think this one is the best fun ever,' said Milo.

However, after a while even Milo grew tired of bouncing, and it was so incredibly noisy, what with the screams of delight and laughter, and the Saucepan Man's clanging, and the clock chiming, that they all decided to go back down the tree for a rest at Silky's house.

'It's always better to leave a land early. Watch out if you ever feel the wind blowing and the ground rocks beneath your feet. It means you're in danger of being trapped there for ever!' Silky warned.

The clock chimed even louder, as if it was an alarm.

'You must try very hard not to chime even once when we're home to give our ears a rest,' said Silky, picking up her clock and giving it an affectionate little tap.

It giggled and chimed a lot more, though it put its tiny arms over its mouth to try to stifle the sound.

Silky's neat pretty house seemed wonderfully still and silent after the crazy Land of Bouncy Castles. The branches near her home were sprouting raspberries now. Silky served them in small glass bowls, lightly sprinkled with sugar and topped with a whirl of cream. It was a lovely light treat and a pleasure to eat it sitting down, not bouncing about.

Pippin ate his in three licks and a big swallow and then looked at Silky hopefully.

'Did I hear you mention honey cakes?' he asked.

'Really, Pippin, you'll give yourself hiccups,' said Silky, but she reached for her cake tin, opened the lid and handed them round.

They were little golden cakes each with a tiny marzipan bee on the top. Mia and Birdy put their bees into their pockets, wanting to keep them. When they all bit into their cakes there was a surprising humming sound, and then the sweetest taste of honey spread over their tongues.

'Oh, I like honey cakes as much as fairy cakes,

maybe even more,' said Birdy, eyeing the tin hopefully.

'Don't be greedy, Birdy,' said Mia, though she'd have loved another one too. 'Don't forget we've got to eat lunch quite soon after we get home.'

Pippin was lolling against her. She felt him tense.

'Pippin? What's the matter?' said Mia.

He didn't answer. She could feel him trembling.

'It's home,' he whispered. 'I haven't got one! This is Silky's home and Moonface has his home and you and Milo and Birdy have your home. I wish I had a home!'

Mia pulled him on to her lap. 'Oh, you poor little thing. Don't worry. You can come home with us!' she said.

'Oh, *yes*!' said Birdy. 'And you can sleep up in my attic room and we can watch out of my window together for when Silky comes to wave to us!'

'And Mum's just bought a whole jar of honey, so you can have lots of treats,' said Milo eagerly. 'I'll even pretend it's me that's eaten it all. She always calls me the human dustbin!'

'You can be our very own special pet!' said Birdy.

'Couldn't I be a chum instead?' Pippin asked.

'Yes, *three* children and their chum!' Birdy sang to the tune of the Saucepan Man's silly song.

'It will be magic!' said Milo.

They made their way back through the Enchanted Wood, Silky kindly flying ahead so they wouldn't get lost.

'Magic!' Milo repeated, but he started to feel doubtful.

Was Pippin a real bear or a magic one? It was clear enough that Silky and Moonface and all the other folk of the Faraway Tree were magical and meant them no harm. Pippin was adorable now, but if he was a real bear he'd become highly dangerous as he grew up. Milo was certain that Mum and Dad wouldn't let him stay with them then, even if they kept him in a big cage – and that was a terrible thought in itself. They probably wouldn't let him stay with them even now, when he was just a little cub.

He thought it through carefully. They'd phone up the nearest zoo and see if a cub had escaped. They'd find a vet, maybe call in the police. Pippin would be taken away from them no matter how they pleaded.

'We'll have to keep Pippin hidden,' he said, as they waved goodbye to Silky and jumped over the ditch, back to the small lane. 'We'll have to smuggle him indoors somehow so Mum and Dad don't see him.'

'But they'll love him!' said Birdy.

'They'll think he might be dangerous,' said Milo. 'Won't they, Mia?'

She knew he was right, but she was irritated all the same.

'Why do you always have to be so *sensible*?' she said.

'Well, somebody's got to be. And I'm the oldest. Which is the worst position in the family, because I get blamed if anything goes wrong,' said Milo.

'You try being in the middle!' said Mia. 'You're not special like the oldest or the youngest, you're just the one who's nothing.'

'What about me? I'm the youngest and you two get to boss me about all the time,' said Birdy.

'I'm not anything,' said Pippin in a very small voice. 'I can't remember if I've got a brother or a sister or a mother or a father. I haven't got anyone!'

'You've got *us*,' said Mia fiercely. 'You're our Pippin and we're going to look after you, and you'll be the happiest, most loved bear in the whole world.'

Smuggling Pippin into the house was relatively easy. Birdy burst into the kitchen and told Mum and Dad some preposterous story about beating Mia *and* Milo and coming first in all the races, and Milo said she was a little fibber and chased her all round the kitchen to tickle her – while Mia charged upstairs with Pippin, taking him right up to Birdy's attic bedroom.

'Now, you'll have to stay here for just a while, but I'll bring you up a big honey sandwich as soon as I can. If you feel sleepy, you can curl up in Birdy's bed. She's got lots of books – you can look at the pictures because I don't suppose you can read yet. Or she's got her wax crayons. You can try making a picture yourself. OK?'

Pippin didn't look very certain, but Mia had to

leave him there and dash back downstairs before her parents started asking where she'd got to. When Birdy and Milo had calmed down Mum started asking them what they'd like to do today.

'We wondered if you'd like to explore some of the villages? Or go on another picnic?' she said. 'Or apparently there's a small amusement park with a bouncy castle. Would you like to go there?'

'I think I've gone off bouncy castles,' said Mia. 'What I'd really like to do is stay here, because it's so lovely. And maybe play races in the lane.'

'I'd like that too,' said Milo.

'And me! I bet I'll win again,' said Birdy.

'You children and your races,' said Mum. 'Well, it suits me, because what *I'd* really like to do is lie in a deckchair in the garden with my book.'

'And I've found a whole pile of huge logs in the garden shed,' said Dad. 'I thought I'd try my hand at a bit of wood carving. That's what *I'd* really like to do.'

'Well, let's all have a staying-at-home day,' said Mum. 'Just don't tire yourself out running up and down, kids. And don't go running into those woods, all right? Promise?'

The children looked stricken.

'Oh, Mum, as if!' said Milo quickly.

'Of course we won't,' said Mia.

'Mmm,' said Birdy worriedly.

When they went up the stairs she whispered, 'Have we told a proper fib?'

'No, because we won't *run* into the Enchanted Wood. We'll walk, right?' said Mia.

'*I* didn't promise,' said Milo.

'Neither did we,' said Mia. 'We didn't actually say the word, did we, Birdy?'

'No we didn't,' said Birdy. 'Look, if Pippin is sharing my bedroom, that means he's mine now, doesn't it?'

'No, he's mine! I comforted him first and I'm the one who carries him around,' said Mia.

'He's *ours*,' said Milo. 'Though didn't Silky say you shouldn't own an animal anyway?'

'That was unicorns. We're talking about a little helpless baby bear,' said Mia.

They hurried up to Birdy's room – and found the little helpless baby bear had been creating havoc, though they'd only been gone five minutes. He had scribbled brown wax crayon all over one white wall, he'd torn two of Birdy's books and he'd thrown all the bedclothes in a heap in one corner.

'Oh, no!' Birdy cried in horror. 'You bad boy!'

'Are you all right, kids?' Mum called from downstairs. 'Milo, what are you doing to your sister?'

'Nothing!' said Milo indignantly.

'We're just playing, Mum,' Mia called.

'*I'm* not going to take the blame for all this mess!' said Milo.

'Pippin didn't *mean* to make a mess. He just doesn't understand houses yet. He's only little,' said Mia.

'I'm little, and I don't scribble on the walls and tear my books,' said Birdy. 'It's not fair – Mum will think *I* did it and she'll be ever so cross.'

Pippin cowered in a corner, quivering. 'I didn't mean to be bad!' he said in a tiny voice.

'I know,' said Mia, crouching down and cuddling

him. 'But you mustn't ever scribble on walls or tear books again, OK?'

'But you told me to make a picture and I did. It's the Faraway Tree,' said Pippin, pointing to the big brown scribble. 'And you said I could look at the pictures in the books so I tore the pages out to see them properly.'

'Oh, I see!' said Mia. 'There now. It was just a silly misunderstanding. You're not a bad bear at all.'

'I might be a little bit bad,' Pippin whispered, peering backwards at the heap of bedclothes in the corner.

'Yes, why did you toss all my bedclothes on the floor?' said Birdy, starting to gather them up. Then she stopped, horrified. She picked up a floppy turquoise leaf-shaped object. 'Look!' she screamed.

'Sh, Birdy, or Mum will think I'm being mean to you again!' Milo hissed. 'What's that weird, furry thing?'

'It's Gilbert's *ear*!' said Birdy, clutching it to her chest. She looked at Pippin. 'What have you done to him? Where's the rest of him? Have you *eaten* him?'

Mia held Pippin at arm's length. He hung his head guiltily.

'Pippin!' she said, horrified.

'I found the big blue wolfie thing in Birdy's bed. He looked like he might bite me, so I bit him first and his ear came off. But I didn't eat it because it's much too fluffy and tickled my throat,' Pippin whispered.

'So where *is* he?' Birdy cried.

'I captured him and put the bedclothes over him to keep him prisoner,' said Pippin.

Milo gathered up the rest of the bedclothes. There was Gilbert, upside down, looking very bedraggled and upset.

'Oh, poor, poor Gilbert!' said Birdy, snatching him up. 'Your face looks all lopsided now with only one ear, but I still love you very much!'

'Don't let him bite me back!' said Pippin, clutching Mia.

'He can't bite you because he's not real,' she said.

'He *is* real,' said Birdy. 'And he's hurting a lot!'

'I think Mum's got a sewing kit. I'll see if I can sneak it out of her room. Then I'll see if I can sew his ear back on. I can only do cross-stitch, but Gilbert won't mind,' said Mia.

'And you make your bed again, Birdy, while I get my flannel from the bathroom to try to rub off all that brown scribble,' said Milo. He looked at Pippin. 'And you sit there in the corner, little bear, and do nothing at all!'

Pippin did his best to behave himself. But he

didn't understand what you should and shouldn't do in a bedroom. He felt a sudden urge to do a wee. And so he did, right there on the floorboards.

'Pippin!' said Birdy, horrified. It was also so funny that it made her giggle hysterically.

Milo didn't find it at all funny because he had to do his best to mop it up – though *not* with his flannel. Mia was very glad she could sew. She made rather a good job of Gilbert's ear, making it stick up at a jaunty angle, as if he were very happy. Birdy was delighted, and even Pippin stopped glaring at him, though he gave him an occasional poke with his paw.

When Mum was lying in her deckchair Mia dashed down to the kitchen and made the honey sandwich she'd promised. Pippin was very enthusiastic, finished it in three big mouthfuls and then gave her lots of sticky kisses.

'Why didn't you bring us a honey sandwich too?' said Birdy. 'I really like honey sandwiches.'

'I don't see why you're rewarding him for making such a mess,' said Milo.

'He didn't mean to. He just doesn't know any

better,' said Mia.

'Well, you're the one who's meant to be good with animals. Why don't you start trying to train him?' said Milo, scrubbing wearily.

Mia did her best. She introduced Pippin to the bathroom. He seemed to think it was a magnificent source of drinking water. He drank the water from the basin and the bath tap. He tried hard to drink the water from the toilet too, but Mia had a firm grip on him and stopped him just in time. He couldn't seem to grasp how to use the toilet for its proper purpose. He nodded obligingly and promised Mia he'd do his best to remember, but when he felt the urge again he forgot to lift the lid and made a terrible mess.

'He's only a little baby, remember?' said Mia, taking her turn at mopping.

'I didn't ever do that when I was a little baby,' said Birdy, not quite accurately. 'Hey, Pippin, do you want to play Mothers and Fathers and pretend that you're *my* little baby?'

Pippin wasn't sure, but he decided to go along with this idea as he really wanted to please the children. He didn't realise this would involve Birdy dressing him up in her nightie. He felt very silly indeed, especially when Milo laughed at him. He tried to pull the nightie off, forgetting his paws were quite sharp.

'You've torn my nightie!' Birdy wailed. 'Mum will blame me now!'

'I'll sew it up for you,' Mia said, though she wasn't sure how she could tackle such a big rip. It was beginning to be clear to her that it wasn't really working having Pippin live in their cottage. She could try to train him as Milo suggested, but it wasn't really fair on him. Pippin was a wild bear cub, not a baby human.

It was even clearer to Milo that living with Pippin was a disaster. When he'd finished mopping and scrubbing at long last he went downstairs and asked Dad if he could look something up on his computer. He asked Google where black bears lived.

'Aha!' said Milo, rushing back upstairs. 'Bears like Pippin live in hollow trees! And we all know a perfect hollow tree, don't we? It's obvious! The

Faraway Tree!'

'Could I live with Silky?' Pippin asked hopefully.

'Probably not a good idea, as she's got such a neat, pretty little home,' said Milo. 'I know you don't mean to, but you make an awful mess, Pippin.'

'What about Moonface? He doesn't mind messes,' said Pippin.

'That's not going to work either!' said Mia. 'He makes enough mess all by himself. How about us finding you your own den in the tree? We'll line it with leaves and make it really cosy for you. Silky and Moonface will look after you and we'll come and see you every day – with a special honey sandwich.'

'*Two* honey sandwiches?' asked Pippin. 'Maybe more? Lots and lots and lots?'

But he was only teasing. He was smiling. 'I think I'd really, really like to live in the Faraway Tree.'

CHAPTER NINE

THE CHILDREN managed to smuggle Pippin back into the Enchanted Wood that day, this time hidden under Birdy's fairy princess cloak.

'But don't you dare tear it!' said Birdy.

'I won't! I like the way it feels,' said Pippin, rubbing his furry cheek against the smooth velvet.

'You're getting it all sticky now,' Birdy muttered, but she managed to be stoical about it.

They found their way to the Faraway Tree in a matter of minutes, the trees obligingly pointing the right way again. The Angry Pixie had returned from the Land of Bouncy Castles, but was still in such a good mood that he simply waved to them cheerily. Dame Washalot was obviously back too, because they heard a sudden swooshing sound from up above. They managed to flatten themselves against the trunk and avoid the waterfall of soapsuds – though perhaps Pippin could have benefited from a thorough bath.

Silky was in too and delighted to see them. She thought at first they were wanting Pippin to live with her, and she was very gracious, but when she realised they were trying to find Pippin his own little home she was even more delighted.

'I know exactly the right place! Woodpecker Cottage!' she said.

'I'm not sure I like woodpeckers,' said Pippin. 'They might mistake me for a piece of wood and peck me!'

'They've all flown away because people complained about the noise of their constant pecking. The Angry Pixie was especially cross because he said they seemed to be drumming right above his head and he couldn't get a wink of sleep. Their cottage has been empty for a week or two. I'm afraid it's very small – but then you're a very small bear, Pippin. Come and see if you like it,' said Silky.

It was a very basic cottage, with a battered door off its hinges, no furniture to speak of and all in all seemed very dark and gloomy – but Pippin clapped his paws.

'I like it very much!' he said. 'And I'll have you as my neighbour, Silky!'

Everyone set to work to improve the cottage. Dame Washalot popped down the tree and gave it a good scrubbing. The Angry Pixie put the door back on its hinges. The children picked hundreds of big green leaves from the tree to make a very soft carpet. Moonface donated several cushions from his slippery-slip and Silky set to work and knitted a beautiful blanket. Mr Watzisname donated a pot of barely used paint and a couple of brushes so that Milo and Mia could paint the newly fixed door a fresh leafy green. Birdy wanted to help too, but when they let her have a go she managed to paint herself more than the door.

'You sit in the corner and amuse Pippin,' Mia ordered.

The Saucepan Man came clanking down the tree and gave Pippin his own small saucepan and kettle. Pippin didn't have a stove and was too young to be trusted with boiling anything anyway, but he thought they made splendid ornaments and put them proudly on his mantelpiece. Silky's clock came running in on his spindly legs, holding hands with a tiny alarm clock who could barely toddle.

'But he can tell the time perfectly. Come on, youngster, show them what you can do,' he said.

The tiny alarm clock piped, 'Wake up time! Breakfast time! Snack time! Lunchtime! Nap time! Another snack time! Teatime! Suppertime! Bedtime! Midnight snack time! Sleep time!' and then he rang his alarm surprisingly loudly. He made them all jump and laughed so much he tipped over.

Pippin laughed too, seized the alarm clock's tiny hands and danced around the room with him.

'There! Now you've got a clock to keep you company too,' said Silky. 'Let's all have a party at my house to celebrate you coming to live at the Faraway Tree, Pippin!'

They all squeezed into Silky's little house – Pippin and Milo and Mia and Birdy, Moonface and Dame Washalot, the Angry Pixie and the Saucepan Man and Mr Watzisname, both talking clocks and a scurry of squirrels. The tree was growing cherries now – beautiful big, ripe cherries, red and yellow and black cherries bursting with juice. The squirrels gathered huge bowlfuls of cherries and expertly removed their stones with their tiny claws. Silky made them all cherryade to drink and sugared doughnuts, each with a very large dollop of cherry jam inside.

They all grew rather sticky, especially Pippin, but Dame Washalot obligingly gave them all a good wipe when they were finished. Pippin and the squirrels all squirmed when their paws and faces got a thorough scrubbing, but they were in such a good mood that nobody protested.

The squirrels grew a little boisterous after a while and started throwing cherry stones at each

other. Pippin thought this tremendous fun and joined in enthusiastically.

'Perhaps we'd better take the party somewhere else now,' said Moonface, as cherry stones hurtled through the air and all Silky's pretty vases and ornaments were under attack. 'Shall we have one last frolic in the Land of Bouncy Castles?'

The Saucepan Man and Mr Watzisname and the Angry Pixie all cheered and declared this an excellent idea. They invited Dame Washalot to go with them. She giggled girlishly and agreed.

'Are you coming too, Silky?' she asked.

'Perhaps I'll pop up later,' she said. 'I think I'll make a batch of honey cakes first just in case Pippin gets peckish his first night here.'

'I do love you, Silky!' said Pippin.

He gave her a big kiss, and then he scampered around thanking everyone for helping him turn Woodpecker Cottage into such a cosy new home. He gave Milo and Mia and Birdy a special kiss too.

'You were so kind to take me to your home and I liked living with you very much indeed, but it wasn't *quite* as nice as having my own house here,' he said.

The children felt a little sad that he wasn't going to be their own bear now, especially Mia, but they could see this was a much better solution. Pippin and all his new squirrel friends ran up the tree to the Land of Bouncy Castles, chattering excitedly, while the two clocks had a competition to see who could chime the longest and loudest.

It was very quiet and peaceful when they'd all gone.

'Don't you three want to go and have another bounce too?' Silky asked, giving them each another cherry doughnut.

'Maybe,' said Milo. He adored the Land of Bouncy Castles, and it was very tempting, but he was feeling very full now, and rather tired too.

'Perhaps not,' said Mia, rubbing her tummy and yawning.

Birdy simply hiccupped.

'I think we'd better go back to our home,' said Milo.

They took the quick route down the Faraway Tree, sliding down on Moonface's slippery-slip, and then threaded their way through the trees. They still weren't quite sure where they were going, but their feet seemed to have remembered all by themselves this time.

Mum was still reading her book in the garden. Dad was fashioning something tall with pieces sticking out at either side.

'What's that, Dad?' Milo asked.

'I'm not quite sure yet,' said Dad.

'It's a man!' said Birdy. 'A giant man. Look, those are his great arms reaching out to grab you!'

'He's a giant insect man then, because he's got lots of arms,' said Mia.

'I'm going to tickle him under one of his arms,' said Birdy, giggling. She was still hiccupping and made a very loud noise.

'Birdy!' said Mum.

'I'm not Birdy, I'm a fairy princess,' said Birdy, spreading out her cloak and whirling round, sticking out one leg. She was trying to be as dainty as Silky – but failing miserably. 'Will you play fairy princesses with me, Mia?'

'No, I absolutely hate being a fairy princess,' said Mia. 'They just faff around in their castles, fussing about whether they're pretty. I'd sooner rush around fighting battles.'

'Silky doesn't faff, whatever that is. She flies around and has adventures,' said Birdy, raising her arms and pretending to fly round the garden.

'Birdy!' said Milo sharply.

Birdy clapped her hand over her mouth, realising what she'd just said.

'Who's Silky?' Mum asked.

Birdy's eyes grew round as she tried to think what to say.

'Oh, she's Birdy's new pretend friend,' Mia said quickly. 'You know what she's like.'

'Ah!' said Mum fondly. 'I remember when you had an imaginary horse, Mia. You always pretended you were riding him. You looked so sweet.'

'Yeah, I remember too. You didn't look sweet, Mia, you looked bonkers galloping about,' said Milo.

'Hey, Milo, stop teasing your sister. I remember when you were little and you used to rush around with your plastic sword slaying pretend dragons,' said Dad, chuckling.

'That was when I was very, very little, only about two,' said Milo loftily. 'Come indoors, Birdy, and I'll get you a drink of water to stop you hiccupping.'

Mia went with them and they had an earnest whispered conversation.

'You mustn't ever start going on about Silky, Birdy, you *know* that,' said Milo.

'I know, I know, but I forgot,' said Birdy. 'And I get mixed up sometimes between my own pretend games and the Faraway Tree ones. They are real, aren't they?'

'Of course they're real,' said Mia, but when she thought about riding like the wind for many miles on the back of a wild unicorn it didn't actually seem very likely. 'Unless – do you think we might be dreaming the Enchanted Wood?'

'But we couldn't all three be dreaming the same dream,' said Milo. 'And look at this bruise on my leg. I got that when I bumped into the Saucepan Man in the refreshment bouncy castle. His saucepans aren't half hard! But it was such fun though, wasn't it? I wish we *had* gone back again now.'

'I don't want to go back there. My insides still feel all shaken up,' said Birdy.

'I don't think all those naughty little squirrels are going to be a good influence on Pippin,' said Mia. 'I do hope he's all right living up the Faraway Tree with no one properly looking after him. I wish we'd kept him now.'

'There's no way we're having Pippin back with us,' said Milo firmly. His hands were still sore after all the scrubbing. 'Pippin's part of the Enchanted Wood, but he's definitely real, isn't he?'

'Yes, he is,' said Birdy, sighing. 'He's broken my brown wax crayon into bits. I wanted to try to draw the Faraway Tree and now I can't.'

'You could colour it in red and pretend it's growing lots and lots of apples. Cox's Orange Pippins,' said Mia. 'Silky will check up on Pippin and make sure he's all right, won't she?'

'Of course she will,' said Milo.

'I'll ask her if she flies past my window tonight,' said Birdy.

She tried extra hard to stay awake this time, though she was very tired. She was actually dozing while she stood waiting at the window, her head resting on the pane, when she dreamt she saw a golden light. She opened her eyes – and there was Silky, hovering in the air, smiling at her.

Birdy jumped up and down excitedly, suddenly wide awake, and Silky waved and blew kisses at her.

'Is Pippin all right?' Birdy hissed.

Silky nodded. She put her head on one side and shut her eyes, miming a little bear fast asleep.

Then she said something else, pointing behind Birdy at something on the floor.

'What?' said Birdy, looking round. Silky seemed to be indicating the pile of clothes on the rug where Birdy had undressed. 'Oh, dear, are you telling me to hang my clothes up? I'm not quite as untidy as Moonface, am I?'

Silky shook her head, smiling, but she was still pointing, seemingly at Birdy's fairy princess cloak.

'*Wear your princess cloak tomorrow!*' Silky mouthed. '*And do you have a princess dress?*'

'Yes, a very pretty blue one. And I have a silver crown! Well, it's not real silver, but it's still very shiny,' said Birdy.

'Wear them all!' said Silky, and then she blew Birdy another kiss and flew away.

Birdy rushed down to Milo and Mia's room.

They were both asleep, Milo spreadeagled on his back, Mia tucked into a little ball.

'Mia, Mia, wake up!' said Birdy, shaking her.

'Pippin?' Mia murmured.

'He's fine. Silky says he's fast asleep,' said Birdy.

'So am I,' said Mia.

'No, wake up and listen! Silky wants me to wear my fairy princess dress and cloak tomorrow, even the crown. I wonder why? Do you think it's her birthday? Or does she just think I'll look pretty in it?' Birdy asked.

'Mmm,' said Mia, who really had gone back to sleep.

Birdy sighed and went back upstairs. She took Gilbert into bed with her and stroked his newly attached ear tenderly, hoping he felt better now. Then she went to sleep herself.

When she woke up the next morning she washed very thoroughly, and put on her fairy princess outfit, even the special sparkly shoes with little heels, though they were rather too small for her now. She tried to put on her crown, squashing her curls down underneath it. They were too bouncy, so the crown kept wobbling.

Dad was in the kitchen, starting to make breakfast.

'Oh, my! Hello, Fairy Princess!' he said, pretending to curtsey.

'Don't be daft, Dad!' said Birdy, giggling. 'Is Mum up? I need her to fix my hair in really neat bunches, so I can wear my crown in between them.'

'Mum's in the garden picking flowers,' said Dad.

Birdy ran out to find her. Her shoes weren't designed for running, and she staggered rather dramatically.

'Whoops!' said Mum, catching her. 'My goodness, I've caught a princess. Come and choose a bouquet for your breakfast table, Your Majesty! Roses or forget-me-nots?'

'Both, please!' said Birdy happily. Mum and Dad were so much better at playing pretend games with her than Milo and Mia.

They stared at her scornfully when they came down to breakfast themselves.

'What on earth have you got that silly old princess outfit on for? You don't need your cloak today!' said Mia.

'And how can you run races in those daft shoes?' said Milo.

'Princesses can do anything they want,' said Birdy loftily. 'Do you like my hair, Mia?'

Mum had tied it up in two bunches, anchored with silver scrunchies that matched Birdy's crown. She had even stuck a rosebud each side, much to Birdy's approval.

'Do you want bunches too, Mia?' Mum asked.

'Noooo, thanks, Mum,' she said.

'What about you, big guy?' Dad joked to Milo. 'Do you fancy bunches?'

'Oh, ha, ha, Dad,' he said. 'Birdy, stop prancing about in your princess stuff. Go and change into your shorts and sandals.'

'You can't tell me what to do – I'm a princess,' said Birdy. 'And I'm keeping my princess outfit on today because it looks pretty and Silky flew past my window and told me to wear it, so there.'

Milo froze.

'Your *pretend friend* Silky?' Mia said quickly.

'Oh, that one. The one you make up, Birdy?' said Milo.

'Yes, my special friend who likes me best and tells me secrets,' said Birdy smugly.

'Well, I'm your special mum and I say you can keep your princess outfit on, Birdy, but I think you'd better change into your sandals before you twist both your ankles or fall flat on your face,' said Mum.

'And I'm your special sister and I say princess shoes are useless if you want to climb trees!' Mia whispered.

Birdy sighed, but changed into her sandals without making any more fuss. They were out of the back gate in two minutes.

'Good girl, Birdy. Come on, let's see how Pippin is,' Mia said, leaping over the ditch. 'Wow, did you see how high I jumped? Maybe if the Land of Unicorns ever comes back, I could try sailing over hedges on my wild unicorn.'

'If it's back today, then *my* little unicorn might pull my silver princess carriage,' said Birdy, skipping over the ditch in her old sandals, secretly relieved to be in comfy shoes again.

'You girls!' said Milo, forging ahead. 'I liked the Land of Bouncy Castles best. I want it to be a *fun* land where we all have a good laugh.'

Pippin was having his breakfast at Silky's house. She was wearing a checked apron. She'd made him a bowl of porridge, creamy and delicious but ordinary enough, but the golden syrup he poured on top was magical. As soon as it landed on top of the porridge, it spread itself around, making a special picture. First it turned itself into a little golden bear cub waving at Pippin. The small syrupy arm actually moved sideways. When he'd spooned it up eagerly Silky let him have another pour. This time it was a picture of the little bear cub splashing in a bathtub, with specks of syrup flying up out of the porridge. Pippin was allowed one more pour and showed the children the picture of a little bear standing on his paws, waggling his back legs comically backwards and forwards.

The children all laughed and Pippin ate the syrupy bear quickly, smacking his lips in appreciation.

'How does the syrup *do* that, Silky?' Mia asked, fascinated.

'It's my own special sort,' said Silky. 'It's non-stick too – an added bonus!'

'Just as well, because I'm wearing my princess dress, just as you told me to,' said Birdy, holding out the skirts of her dress and twirling round.

'You look wonderful too,' said Silky. 'And I love the way your hair's styled! Perhaps you could show me how to do my hair like that? It keeps getting in the way when I cook.'

'Our mum does it for us, but I think I could show you,' said Mia.

'Per-lease don't let's waste time playing hairdressers!' said Milo. 'I don't suppose there's any of that magic syrup left?' he added hopefully.

Silky made them three bowls of porridge and three individual jugs of syrup. They'd only just had their breakfast at home, but they weren't going to miss this opportunity! Milo's syrup turned into a picture of a boy running, his arms flying upwards, his racing feet making little dents in the porridge. Mia's syrup became a unicorn who arched his neck and pointed his long horn at her. Birdy's syrup showed a small girl who sprouted wings and actually flew round the bowl.

'Oh, this is so wonderful! Can't we just stay here at Silky's and see syrup pictures?' said Birdy.

'I think you'll like the land up above today,

195

Birdy,' said Silky. 'I'm just going to go and get ready to go there.'

She disappeared behind a screen and started changing her clothes. She was only gone for a few seconds – but when she bobbed back again she was utterly transformed. She was wearing a dazzling pale-pink dress with little silver thread flowers. Her wings were a deeper shade of pink with silver tips. She wore dainty silver shoes with high heels and a sparkling crystal crown on her long fair hair.

The children and Pippin stared at her.

'You look like a real princess!' Birdy said in awe.

Silky blushed, her cheeks as pink as her wings. 'We're going up to the Land of Princesses,' she said.

'What?' said Milo.

'And Princes too,' said Silky. 'Saucepan came last night to see if Pippin would like to have a specially small saucepan to wear as a hat—'

'And I wanted one dreadfully,' Pippin interrupted. 'But Silky said I might wedge it on too hard and get it stuck for ever. I wouldn't mind – it would look funny!'

'And while we were having a glass of blackberry wine together he told me that he'd heard the Land of Princes and Princesses would be here today,' Silky finished.

'Oh, how lovely!' said Birdy, jumping up and down and nearly tripping over her own princess dress.

Milo and Mia looked at each other, thinking this land sounded anything *but* lovely. Milo felt ill at the thought of hundreds of princes milling about in those silly tunics and embarrassing tights, though he didn't mind the idea of princesses so much. He hoped one might need rescuing from a dragon. He longed to see a real dragon. Mia was totally appalled. She didn't mind the idea of brave princes fighting battles, but she detested the thought of princesses prancing around in crowns and party frocks. She was very much a jeans sort of girl.

However, Birdy was so excited that it seemed mean not to go there. Milo and Mia knew that Silky would look after Birdy, but she was their little sister after all, and their responsibility.

'Let's go then,' said Milo.

'Just for a quick peep,' said Mia.

'We'll call for Moonface. I'm sure he wouldn't want to miss the chance of going there,' said Silky.

Moonface didn't seem very keen.

'I'm not sure I've got time today,' he said. 'The red squirrel is still very cross with me for shrinking and stretching Tipkin so dramatically, and won't work for me as my cushion collector any more. I'm tired of climbing up and down the Faraway Tree collecting the cushions myself every time someone has a ride down the slippery-slip. I've promised all the other squirrels a decent week's wages with two Toffee Shocks a day as a bonus, but none of them are interested. I suppose I'll have to fall back on rabbits, but they're never reliable, forever darting off down burrows when they're most needed.'

'Why don't you close the slippery-slip just for the day?' said Silky. 'Come on, Moonface, it'll be such fun. I expect there will be a ball and I'd love you to be my dance partner.'

'Oh, Silky, you know I'm not much of a dancer.

You go with the children and young Pippin. Milo can be your partner!'

Milo went hot with embarrassment at the idea, but didn't want to hurt Silky's feelings with an outright refusal.

'*I'll* be your partner, Silky! I love dancing up and down!' said Pippin, leaping about.

This wasn't really Silky's style of dancing at all, but she smiled at him gratefully.

They climbed the Faraway Tree to the ladder reaching up into the cloud. Birdy was very much last, because it was extremely difficult climbing in her long princess dress, and her arms kept getting stuck in her cloak. She was glad now that she'd worn her sandals – her princess heels would have slipped dangerously. Silky had no problem in her own beautiful shoes – she flew upwards, slowly and gracefully, her crystal shoes neatly pointed.

'Wait for me!' Birdy kept shouting.

Milo hung back to help her, but Birdy complained he was pushing her, so he decided he wouldn't bother. Birdy hauled herself up the ladder at last, hot and cross – but when she poked her crowned head through the cloud she blinked in astonishment and delight.

CHAPTER TEN

BIRDY WOULD have climbed ten trees this high to see such a sight. She had been expecting a building rather like a bouncy castle, but made out of stone or brick. This gleaming palace was very different. It was made of marble and glowed snow-white in the brilliant sunshine. It had too many towers for Birdy to count, each with many windows. People were leaning out, watching what was happening down below, on the green sward. Many folk were gathered in an immense viewing area. There were two large gold thrones for an elderly couple wearing long purple cloaks edged with fur in spite of the heat.

The lady had such an elaborate hairstyle that her crown teetered precariously right at the top. The gentleman wore a crown too, and had a long white beard that had been carefully plaited and tied with a gold chain. They were clearly the queen and king of this royal land.

Two princely knights in silver armour were mounted on huge horses at either end of the grass arena. Both knights held very long steel poles with pointed ends. At a sudden command they started thundering towards each other on their horses, the poles held high. They both scored glancing blows at their opponents, but stayed seated. The crowd roared and clapped. The knights reined in their horses and dismounted while pages rushed to sponge the animals and give their masters a swig of wine from golden goblets.

'Why are they fighting?' Birdy asked, jumping out of the cloud on to the bright grass.

'It's called jousting,' said Milo. 'It's like a pretend battle to see who can knock the other one off his horse. The armour stops them getting hurt. They must be incredibly strong!'

These weren't foppish princes lolling around in fancy clothes. Milo was very impressed. So was Mia, gazing at their white steeds.

'Their horses are the really strong ones,' she said. 'They're incredible! Not as wonderful as the wild unicorn of course, but almost. I wonder if ladies are ever allowed to be knights?'

'You don't get lady knights,' said Milo.

'I could be the first,' said Mia determinedly.

The three children, Silky and Pippin hurried nearer to the jousting place, so they had a clearer view. There were entertainers to amuse the crowd while the knights and their steeds had a rest. A man played bagpipes, several jugglers tossed umpteen balls in the air and a woman dressed like a ballet dancer led a bear around on a gold chain, encouraging it to dance with her.

'Oh, the poor bear!' said Mia, picking Pippin up protectively.

The knights had great plumes of coloured feathers on their headpieces. Each plucked one from his helmet. The knight with blue feathers presented one to a pretty princess in an azure-blue dress.

'Oh, I'm wearing blue too! Why couldn't he have picked me?' said Birdy, smoothing her crumpled skirt and trying to hide her scuffed sandals.

The knight with deep-pink feathers was looking

round him. There were many ladies wearing all shades of pink in the pavilion, but none seemed to take his fancy. Then he glanced over to the side, towards the children.

'Oh, maybe *he's* going to give me a feather!' said Birdy. 'I've got pink roses in my hair.'

She held her breath as he walked towards her on his pointed armoured feet. But he wasn't looking at her after all. He was looking at Silky, in all her pale-pink beauty. He bowed low in spite of his stiff armour and presented her with his deep-pink feather.

Silky took it and gave him a little curtsey.

'Oh, you lucky thing!' said Birdy, breathing out.

Silky seemed very flattered and held her feather high as the two knights remounted. When they began the next bout the pink knight managed to knock the knight with the blue plumes right off his horse.

They were worried that he might be hurt, but he scrambled to his feet, took his helmet off and bowed low to his contestant, managing to smile.

'Oh, I hope your knight takes his helmet off now, Silky!' said Birdy. 'I want to see if he's really handsome!'

'He's not "my" knight, Birdy,' Silky protested. 'And it doesn't matter if he's handsome or not. It's whether he is kind and brave and valiant.'

'Like Moonface?' said Birdy. 'He's certainly not very handsome, is he?'

'Birdy!' said Mia, giving her a nudge.

'He has a very dear face,' said Silky.

'He's very kind,' said Pippin. 'He's given me his best cushion and three Toffee Shocks.'

'Yes, Moonface is very kind. He certainly makes a fuss of all the little creatures that visit him,' said Silky.

'And is he brave?' Birdy persisted.

Silky had to think hard. 'When the Angry Pixie was in a very bad mood and threw water all over me Moonface said he was very mean and threatened to throw water over *him*,' she said.

'That's quite brave,' said Birdy uncertainly. 'And what was the other thing? Val something?'

'Valiant. I suppose it means courageous, determined, heroic,' said Silky.

Birdy still looked blank.

'Like a superhero, in comics and films,' said Milo. 'Like Spider-Man. Or Batman.'

'I don't know who they are,' said Silky. You didn't get comics or films in the Enchanted Wood. 'But Moonface isn't very keen on spiders and when a bat flew into his room he whizzed down his slippery-slip in a jiffy to get away from it.'

The children giggled. 'Oh, I shouldn't have told you that. Poor Moonface. He's got lots and lots of very good, special qualities,' she said hurriedly.

'Look!' said Pippin, tugging her arm. 'The man in the shining suit and pink feathers is coming over here!'

The sunshine was glinting on the knight's armour. He was very tall and upright and the crowd clapped as he passed them. Men gazed enviously, women fluttered in his wake and children tried to touch his shining armour. He was very gentle with them, holding hands with the smallest. He looked every inch a superhero.

'He's coming to talk to you, Silky!' said Mia.

'Of course he's not,' said Silky, bending her

head – but when she looked up the knight was right in front of her. She curtsied again, graceful as always, though the children saw she was trembling.

The knight took his helmet off, as Birdy had hoped. He was very, very handsome, with a lean, sculpted face, and beautiful brown eyes.

'Prince Hunter at your service, madam,' he said, bowing low to her.

'Madam!' Milo whispered to Mia.

'I know!' Mia murmured.

'A real prince!' said Birdy, tremendously impressed.

'And you must be a real princess,' said Prince Hunter, bowing to her too.

'Yes, I'm Princess Birdy,' she said, attempting a curtsey, but very nearly toppling over sideways.

Prince Hunter gallantly supported her, as if they were about to dance. Birdy misunderstood.

'Are you my partner for the ball?' she asked hopefully.

'I would like to partner both you *and* the lovely Miss Silky,' he said. He turned to Mia. 'And to partner you too,' he added tactfully.

'And me?' Pippin said.

'And you, little dancing bear,' said Prince Hunter, unfazed.

Milo went hot all over, frightened that the prince would expect him to dance too.

'Is there going to be any more jousting?' he asked. 'I'd really much rather watch that if it's OK with you.'

'And me,' said Mia. 'You've got a magnificent horse, Prince Hunter.'

'I'm afraid the jousting tournament is finished for today,' said the prince. 'But if you'd like to go over to the stables, you'll see all the young lads practising in the yard. And I'm sure my page will appreciate a hand with my horse, Stout-Hearted.'

Milo and Mia dithered for a few seconds, exchanging glances. They very much wanted to take up his offer, but knew how much Birdy wanted to go to the ball. They felt they should keep an eye on their little sister when they were in one of the magic lands at the top of the Faraway Tree. Still, she would have Silky with her, and Prince Hunter himself to protect her.

So they agreed, and parted company. Birdy and Silky and Pippin went through the great golden gates of the palace and disappeared among a throng of ball-goers dressed in their finest clothes. Milo and Mia threaded their way through the crowds outside and went towards the huge stabling complex at the side of the palace.

'How will the stable people know we've got Prince Hunter's permission?' said Milo. 'He should have given you one of his pink feathers, Mia!'

'I didn't want one! All this courtly stuff is a bit weird and silly, isn't it?' said Mia, but there was a small part of herself that would have liked to have been presented with a feather too.

It turned out they didn't need any feathers to prove who they were. Prince Hunter's page recognised them.

'Ah, you are friends of the beautiful lady who has stolen my master's heart,' he said, sighing. 'He's so romantic. I do hope he doesn't do anything too impetuous, like asking for her hand in marriage.'

'I don't think he will. They've only just met!' said Milo.

'And anyway, Silky's got a very close friend back at the Faraway Tree,' said Mia. 'She's going back to him at the end of the day.'

The page seemed reassured. He turned to Milo. 'Now, young sir, I expect you'd like to learn the principles of jousting,' he said, leading him over to some young stable lads who were running at each other, waving long sticks in the air. These were nowhere near the size of jousting poles, and were well padded at the ends, so they couldn't really hurt each other, and they all wore painted breastplates as protection.

'I'd love to join in!' said Milo.

'I'll have a go too. It looks great fun,' said Mia.

The page looked a little startled. 'But you are a young lady. Ladies don't joust!' he said.

'Why not?' Mia asked.

'Because ladies are delicate – and besides, their long dresses would hamper them,' said the page.

'I'm not the slightest bit delicate. I'm as tough as old boots,' said Mia. 'And I don't ever wear long dresses.'

'Yes, I can see you're already wearing stout manly garb,' said the page, looking at Mia's jeans. 'Very well, then, madam.'

Mia giggled. 'Thank you. But I'm not really a madam. My name's Mia,' she said. 'And this is my brother, Milo.'

'I am Michael,' said the page. 'I keep the breastplates over here. Let me strap them into place for you.'

They were painted with an ornate letter M to show they belonged to Michael.

'But it's M for Milo too,' said Milo.

'And M for Mia,' said Mia. She was determined to show she was just as good at jousting as Milo – hopefully even better.

She certainly proved fast to learn and her aim with the stick was accurate – but Milo was that little bit taller and stronger, and kept winning each joust. He cheered himself, so relieved

Mia couldn't beat him.

'Don't look cross, Mia. You know you're heaps better at riding than me,' he said.

'I think Stout-Hearted is still feeling fresh. Maybe you'd like to ride him, Madam Mia?' Michael suggested.

He teamed Milo up with another lad his own size to carry on jousting, and took Mia over to Stout-Hearted's stable. He reared his great white head over his wooden stall, trying to get at her.

'He won't hurt you,' Michael said quickly.

'Of course he won't! He's just wanting to say hello,' said Mia, reaching up and stroking him.

Stout-Hearted breathed through his nostrils, greeting her.

'Can I really ride you?' Mia asked him.

'I'll put him on a leading rein,' said Michael.

'I won't need that,' said Mia.

'How much experience have you had?' he asked doubtfully.

In the ordinary world Mia hadn't had any experience whatsoever, but she had ridden bareback for miles in this enchanted world, so she felt totally confident.

'I've ridden a sea unicorn,' she said casually.

'No one can ride a sea unicorn,' said Michael.

'Ask Milo,' said Mia. 'Anyway, I'd love to ride Stout-Hearted.'

Michael insisted on a leading rein at first, especially as he had to help Mia up on to the mounting block and adjust the stirrups for her – but as soon as she was properly on Stout-Hearted's back, it was obvious she knew what she was doing. She clucked gently to him and gave his broad back the softest touch with her trainers and he started trotting along willingly. Mia's light build was a joy after the burden of a full-sized prince in heavy armour. He moved with a spring in his step, and Mia bounced along with him, her back straight, her head held high.

'It's as if you've been riding him all your life,' said Michael, and he took the leading rein off.

Mia rode Stout-Hearted out into the training field, urged him into a gallop and went round and round. The stable boys came out to watch.

'Who *is* that boy with the strange blue trousers?' one of them murmured, confused by Mia's clothing.

'She's my sister,' said Milo proudly.

'You dress like common folk, but you must be a prince and princess in disguise,' said his jousting partner. 'You're both extremely gifted!'

It was so glorious to be admired like this that Milo and Mia stayed a very long time at the stables, but eventually they started to wonder if

Birdy was all right.

'I think Prince Hunter will be dancing with Silky most of the time, and Birdy might be feeling a bit left out,' said Milo.

'She'll be prancing around with Pippin, I bet you,' said Mia, but she started to worry a little too.

They reluctantly thanked Michael, and Milo shook hands with all the stable lads while Mia gave Stout-Hearted a big hug. They left the stables in a glow of admiration – but it was a different matter at the palace gates. The soldiers on guard found their casual clothes very suspicious and were reluctant to let them pass.

'This is nonsense. We are visiting royalty,' said Milo in his grandest voice. 'Prince Hunter is friends with us. He is at the ball already with our sister, Princess Birdy, the Lady Fairy Silky and our bear, Pippin.'

It sounded so ridiculous that Mia couldn't help giggling – but it did the trick. The soldiers immediately stopped guarding their way and bowed.

'Please enter, Your Majesties,' they said, and

even Milo had to press his lips together to stop himself snorting.

They hurried up hundreds of marble steps and went through the huge carved doors. They walked along a long red carpet, sobered now by the grand paintings along the walls and the giant crystal chandeliers hanging from the high ceiling. They heard the sound of distant music.

'It must be from the ballroom,' said Milo.

Mia looked at his sweaty forehead and his old T-shirt. She felt very grubby too and knew she was probably smelling strongly of horse.

'Don't we look a bit too scruffy to go into a ballroom?' she said.

Milo was surprised. Mia didn't usually care what she looked like. He realised she was probably right. Still, they had to go and find Birdy, even if everyone stared at them. They followed the red carpet until they were at the door to the ballroom. The music was the very old-fashioned sort, tinkly and swirly – definitely not the wild-leaping-about kind when it doesn't matter if you don't know what you're doing.

Milo felt anxious. He felt he ought to ask Silky to dance, but knew that if he did, he'd make a complete fool of himself and probably trample on her toes. Mia was worried too. She suddenly felt very small and self-conscious, a horribly uncomfortable feeling.

They clasped hot hands and walked into the ballroom together. They looked for Birdy, but the room was such a dazzle of light and colour, and the room so large, that everything blurred. There seemed to be thousands of people waltzing round and round on the shining dance floor, thousands more sitting around the edges at little gold tables and even thousands of people in the band at the end, playing their hearts out while a small conductor waved his baton wildly in the air.

There was just one couple who stood out, almost as if they had a spotlight on them. It was a tall handsome man in a dark-pink velvet outfit with a golden crown on his head, dancing with a beautiful lady in paler pink, her gossamer wings waving delicately behind her.

A NEW ADVENTURE

'Prince Hunter and Silky!' said Milo.

'She doesn't look like our Silky any more,' said Mia. 'She really looks like a princess.'

'Look at the way she's staring up at him,' said Milo. It was a relief that Silky didn't seem inclined to swap partners, but it worried him all the same. 'I wish Moonface had come with us,' he added.

'Poor little Birdy! She'll be feeling so left out,' said Mia, looking round the room for her. She didn't seem to be sitting at any of the tables. Mia's heart started thumping – but then she spotted her sister, right in the middle of the dance floor. She was twirling about, her crown crooked, her princess dress tucked up, pointing her old sandals as she danced with a small boy around her own age. He was grandly dressed in crimson velvet, though there were smears of ice cream down his front. His crown was crooked too, almost slipping off his pageboy haircut, but it shone brightly, studded with large red stones.

'That crown looks real! I think those stones must be rubies! Birdy's dancing with a real little prince!' said Milo.

'So where's Pippin?' said Mia, anxious all over again.

At last they spotted him in a corner with the dancing bear with the long gold chain. He was still wearing it, but he'd twitched it away from his owner, and he and Pippin were doing handstands together, waggling their back legs in time to the music.

'They're all having fun,' said Milo. He felt so light-hearted that he squeezed Mia's hand. 'Come on – let's dance too.'

'But we can't! We don't know how to dance. We'll look silly and everyone will stare,' said Mia.

'Who cares?' said Milo.

Mia was astonished at his sudden boldness. 'OK then,' she said, thinking he might be bluffing.

But he pulled her right on to the dance floor and started whirling her round until they were both dizzy and breathless.

'This dancing isn't so bad after all,' Mia puffed. 'Though let's whirl the other way now or we'll both fall over!'

They found themselves whirling nearer and nearer Silky and Prince Hunter, who seemed in a world of their own.

'Hi, Silky!' Milo called, but she didn't seem to hear.

'Just look at them! They're gazing into each other's eyes all the time,' said Mia.

'Yes, well, she'll have to stop gazing soon. She'll have to go back to the Faraway Tree by evening or she might find herself whirled right away for ever,' said Milo.

'Well, let's give her a little longer, as she looks so happy,' said Mia. 'And Birdy and Pippin are obviously having fun. So let's have fun too, Milo!'

The band started a comical tune, very different from the sedate waltz they'd been playing. The dancers clapped and then started doing a very silly dance, waving their hands in the air, clutching their knees, tapping their toes to the left and the right, bumping bottoms and then taking their partners by the arm and capering round and round. Milo and Mia had to concentrate at first, because the music was so fast it was difficult to fit everything in, but they soon got the hang of it and were laughing uproariously.

Birdy and her little prince were pretty hopeless at the novelty dance, but didn't care, mostly bumping bottoms and jigging. Pippin and the chained bear simply leapt up and down doing star jumps with the occasional leapfrog for variety.

'Where are Silky and Prince Hunter?' said Milo.

'They're over there, at the table right in the corner. See, they're eating ice cream out of crystal dishes,' said Mia. 'Prince Hunter is obviously too grand for this type of dancing.'

Perhaps she was right, though the actual king and queen had jumped off their thrones and were doing the silly dance themselves, roaring with laughter. It went on for a very long while, because every time the perspiring band slowed down the crowd begged for more. But then lemonade was served in carved jade goblets and there was enough ice cream for everyone.

'Mmm, chocolate, my favourite!' said Milo.

'No, it's strawberry, *my* favourite!' said Mia. 'Yet it's coloured white, like ordinary vanilla.'

'Perhaps it's like Silky's food, and changes in your mouth,' said Milo. 'I hope she learns the recipe – it's delicious.'

They both looked over at the table in the corner – but it was occupied by a giggling couple who were wearing their crystal dishes on their heads like crowns. There was no sign of Silky and Prince Hunter.

'Oh-oh!' said Mia. 'I bet they've gone out into the palace grounds to get a breath of fresh air. It always happens in films. And then they start kissing.'

'Well, Silky can't go kissing anyone else. She's got Moonface back at the Faraway Tree!' Milo said indignantly.

'Yes, I know. But he couldn't be bothered to come with us. And though I like Moonface ever so much I think I'd sooner kiss a handsome prince,' said Mia. 'Actually I'd much sooner kiss a unicorn.'

'You don't really think she's gone off with him, do you?' said Milo.

'Not really,' said Mia, though she wasn't sure.

Milo looked at his watch, but of course it had stopped the moment he'd set foot in the Enchanted Wood.

'How long have we been here, do you think?' he asked. 'It's so difficult to tell. And mornings and afternoons and evenings all seem to get mixed up too. Look out of that window. It's moonlight!'

'Oh, no! Then perhaps they really are kissing!' said Mia.

'And if it's evening here, then maybe the Land of Princes and Princesses *will* move on soon – with us, as well as Silky!' said Milo.

'Come on then – let's round up Birdy and Pippin and go and find Silky and get us all down the ladder quick sharp!' said Mia.

It was a struggle. Birdy was having great fun with the little prince, competing with each other to see who could eat the most ice cream.

'I don't want to go back yet! I'm with my handsome prince and I expect we're going to get married soon and live happily ever after,' said Birdy.

'Oh, Birdy, don't be silly. This is just pretend,' said Mia.

'You're much too young to marry anyway,' said Milo.

'And what about Mum and Dad? Wouldn't you miss them?' said Mia. 'Now come on!'

Pippin was even harder to persuade. He was very attached to the dancing bear, and whimpered when Milo and Mia tried to prise them apart.

'We have to find Silky!' Milo said urgently. 'Now

stop hugging your friend!'

'It's what bears do! Haven't you ever heard of a bear hug?' Pippin protested, but when he thought that Silky was lost he reluctantly came with them.

They hunted everywhere for her, in the palace itself and then all over the grounds, though it was hard to see where they were going by moonlight alone and they didn't have any torches.

'Let's all hold hands so that we don't lose each other!' Milo suggested sensibly, but before they could do so Birdy managed to trip on her trailing princess dress and fell over.

She didn't really hurt herself, but she was tired out and overexcited and burst into tears.

'Oh, Birdy, don't cry!' said Mia, picking her up and giving her a quick hug.

But Birdy cried harder – and suddenly there was Silky, glowing palely in the moonlight, with Prince Hunter beside her.

'What's the matter, Birdy?' Silky said anxiously, running to her.

Birdy had got to that stage of crying when she

couldn't even talk. She ran into Silky's arms and wept on her shoulder. Silky clasped her close and rocked her, while Prince Hunter put his arm round both of them.

'What's happened to Birdy?' Silky asked the children. 'Oh, dear, I should never have left her – but she seemed to be having so much fun dancing.'

'We were all just a bit anxious, wondering where you were,' said Mia.

'But it's all right now,' said Milo. 'We'd just better go back down the Faraway Tree now as it's dark. The land might start to move away!'

'Yes, you're right. You must go back down the ladder now,' said Silky. 'Do you think you can find it? We'll show you where it is, won't we, Prince Hunter?'

'Of course, dear Silky,' he said.

The children were puzzled.

'But – but you're coming too, aren't you, Silky?' said Mia.

Silky shook her head sorrowfully. 'I'm so sorry. I don't want to upset you. I'm so fond of all of you – but I'm afraid I'm not coming back.'

They stared at her. Birdy stopped crying in shock. Pippin put his paw in his mouth.

'What do you mean?' said Milo, though there was no mistaking what she'd said.

'I'm staying here in the Land of Princes and Princesses,' said Silky.

CHAPTER ELEVEN

'SILKY'S GOING to be my princess,' said Prince Hunter
proudly.

'You can't be! Not really! This is just pretend!'
said Birdy.

'It's real for me,' said Silky. 'I didn't mean this to
happen, but it has, and I can't help it. I'm in love with
Prince Hunter.'

'But what about Moonface!' said Milo.

'Oh, dear Moonface,' said Silky, and a tear slid
down her cheek. 'I shall miss him dreadfully. But I
think he'll barely notice I'm gone. I'm sure he'll find
someone else to look after him – or maybe he'll even

learn how to look after himself.'

'He needs *you*, Silky!' said Mia. 'He'll be terribly sad without you. And the Saucepan Man will miss you so much too, and Dame Washalot, and all the squirrels . . . What will happen if Moonface accidentally does a spell wrong again?'

'You mustn't worry, madam,' said Prince Hunter. 'My beloved Silky has told me about her concerns for this strange friend. I will lend him my own enchanter to coach him in the magical arts. I have enough enchantment of my own,' he added, gazing at Silky.

Milo and Mia glanced at each other, pulling faces, but Birdy looked enthralled. Pippin however growled at the prince and bared his teeth, looking as if he was about to bite his shapely ankle.

'Silky!' said Birdy, and she went over to her and took hold of her hand. '*Please* come back! You're my *friend*!'

Silky was weeping now, her cheeks wet, but she gently eased her hand away from Birdy's grip.

'The Land of Princes and Princesses will come

back to the Faraway Tree at some time and then I will come and visit you, dearest Birdy, I promise,' said Silky.

'But that might not be for ages,' said Pippin. 'What will I do if I have a bad dream and can't get back to sleep in my new home?'

'Moonface will comfort you, Pippin. He's very kind and he loves playing with all little creatures,' said Silky. 'Oh, Moonface!' She hid her head in Prince Hunter's chest.

'Silky! Oh, Silky!' a voice cried. It was Moonface himself, running through the trees, stumbling, his jacket unbuttoned, his check trousers torn, his sparse hair tousled.

Silky looked up as he called. Her hands went to her face. She stared at him wildly.

'I've been looking everywhere for you! You've been gone so long I was starting to get worried, so I came here to look for you. I went to the ball to dance with you, but you weren't there, so now I've been all over the garden and I kept falling over in the dark, but what does that matter? I've found you!'

Moonface beamed, his white head almost as bright as the real moon above.

Then he realised Silky was clinging to someone else: a tall handsome man in splendid robes with a crown on his head.

'Who are you? What's going on? Let Silky go!' Moonface cried.

'I am Prince Hunter and Silky has just agreed to be my princess,' said the prince.

'*What?*' said Moonface. He drew himself as upright as he could, though he was still only half Prince Hunter's size. 'What nonsense is this!'

'I'm afraid it's true, Moonface. I'm so sorry. I don't want to hurt you, but it's true,' said Silky.

'I don't want to hurt *you*, dear Silky. You have clearly been enchanted by this dastardly man! I am seriously affronted.' Moonface was trying to talk like a prince himself, but it sounded very strange. 'Take your arm away from her, sir! If you don't let her go, I shall . . . I shall knock you down!'

'Oh, Moonface, please don't try!' said Mia. 'You'll only get hurt!'

'Prince Hunter is so much bigger than you!' Milo pointed out, not very tactfully.

'Silky, stop him!' said Birdy.

'No, hit him, Moonface – and I'll bite him!' said Pippin. He ran at Prince Hunter, growling as ferociously as he could.

Prince Hunter didn't flinch, even when Pippin went for his ankle. He simply moved his long, elegant foot and nudged Pippin away. It wasn't exactly a kick, but it sent the cub rolling.

'Don't you dare attack my little friend!' Moonface cried. He gathered himself together, clenching his fists. 'Move away, Silky!' he commanded, and then he ran full speed at Prince Hunter.

He butted his big round head into Prince Hunter's taut stomach, and hit out with both fists at his manly chest.

'Take that, you varmint!' he cried.

Prince Hunter folded his great arms and actually laughed. It was somehow crueller than fighting Moonface back. It was hard to see colours in the moonlight, but it was clear that poor Moonface was

A NEW ADVENTURE

flushing as crimson as a setting sun.

He charged at Prince Hunter again, who stepped sideways so that Moonface missed him altogether and went crashing to the ground. He went down with such a wallop that it was clear he'd really hurt himself this time.

'Moonface!' Silky cried, rushing to him.

'Leave him alone, you bully!' Mia shouted at Prince Hunter.

'How could you hit someone smaller than yourself?' Milo said furiously.

'Call yourself a prince?' said Birdy.

'I'll tear you to ribbons!' said Pippin.

'You've attacked my dearest friend!' said Silky, kneeling beside Moonface and smoothing his hair.

Prince Hunter looked bewildered, as he hadn't actually attacked Moonface at all – it was quite the other way round.

'I don't wish him any harm, dear Silky. I feel sorry for him,' said Prince Hunter.

'There's no need to feel sorry for me, you great foolish fop!' said Moonface, struggling up again.

'I won't have it!'

He leapt wildly in the air and took another swing at Prince Hunter. By chance his clenched fist collided with the prince's firm chin and his head tilted. His golden crown crashed to the ground.

'Enough!' said Prince Hunter. 'I will not be insulted in this way! That is the royal crown, worn by many princes before me, each and every one of true majestic blood. I'm warning you, little man! Touch me again and I'll fight you back!'

'You can't frighten me!' said Moonface. 'I want to fight! Choose your weapon, sir! Sword, blunderbuss, bare fists?'

Moonface could barely lift a full-sized sword, he didn't even know how to pull the trigger of a blunderbuss and his fist was already bleeding painfully from its contact with Prince Hunter's chin, but he was utterly determined.

'So be it, you silly fool,' said Prince Hunter. 'I will call my page and he will bring weapons for both of us.'

'Stop this!' said Silky desperately, standing

between them. 'How can you both be so silly? You can't fight over me!'

'Then you must choose between us. Would you rather stay in the glorious Land of Princes and Princesses or would you prefer to return to your strange tree?' said Prince Hunter. 'I will free you from your promise to me if you really wish to go back home with this bizarre fellow.'

He picked up his crown, placed it firmly on his head and stood tall and proud, hands on his hips. Moonface stood beside him, tousled and bleeding, half his size. He was trembling.

'Choose, Silky,' he said. He swallowed hard. 'If you really feel you will be happier with this less than charming prince and you want to leave the Magic Faraway Tree, then I can't stop you – though I will miss you very much.'

Milo and Mia and Birdy and Pippin stood still, barely breathing.

Silky looked at Prince Hunter. She looked at Moonface.

'I choose you, Moonface,' she whispered.

Prince Hunter gave her one look, and then turned on his heel and marched off towards the palace.

'Hunter!' Silky called after him. It looked as if she might change her mind.

'He's just make-believe, Silky,' said Birdy insistently.

They all stared after him – and in the strange moonlight he did seem eerily transparent, in spite of his size and bulk. A strong wind made their eyes water. There was a sudden jolt beneath them, the grass rippling a little, the trees swaying.

Moonface clasped Silky. Milo grabbed Birdy, and Mia pulled Pippin up into her arms.

'What's happening? Everything's tilting!' said Milo.

'The land's starting to move! Quick, we must get down the ladder before we're stuck here for ever!' Moonface yelled.

'Where is it?' cried Mia.

'In front of the palace!' said Moonface desperately. 'We must run!'

He tried to lift Silky into his arms, but he had no

strength left. She had to help him along, beating her wings to keep them both upright. Milo gave Birdy a piggyback and Mia told Pippin to hang on tightly, and then they ran. They ran and ran and ran, while the land kept jerking and tilting and the wind grew stronger, so they had to battle against it.

It seemed almost impossible that they would get to the ladder in time. Even when they actually got to the front of the palace they couldn't see it. The grass

had been churned up by the crowds watching the jousting, and now it was wavering up and down so it was like running through a stormy sea.

Pippin spotted the small wooden knobs at the end of the ladder first, barely poking out of the ground.

'The ladder – the ladder! Look, over there!' he shouted, practically deafening Mia.

She ran as fast as she could, but Milo got there first, just as the land tilted so dramatically it seemed just attached by a wisp of cloud. He pushed Birdy down the ladder, reached out his hand, grabbed Mia and Pippin, and pulled them down too.

Silky and Moonface were still staggering a little way away. Milo ran like the wind, grabbed Moonface under the arm, and helped them both. They reached the ladder as the land gave one final jerk, and as they tumbled down it suddenly rose right up in the air and whirled above them, higher and higher until it was almost out of sight.

They all heard a faint regal voice calling one last time, '*Silky!*'

'Hunter!' Silky gasped – and then the land was gone and there was just great silent darkness above the cloud.

The Saucepan Man and Mr Watzisname came rushing to see what the commotion was, and insisted on pulling everyone into their home. Saucepan filled his biggest kettle on the hob of his stove while Mr Watzisname busied himself seating everyone somehow or other, and fetched a sponge to mop Moonface's cuts and bruises.

'Two dear friends in trouble,
Two more, and two more.
Two kettles, bubble, bubble,
Making tea for all four!'

Saucepan sang, as he made tea for everyone, and brought out a tin of fruit cake.

'But there's only one kettle – and there are six friends drinking tea. Actually eight if you count yourself and Mr Watzisname,' said Birdy, counting on her fingers.

'Oh, Birdy, as if it matters,' said Mia, pulling her on to her lap. Pippin was there already, so it was a bit of a squash.

Milo hovered beside Moonface and Silky. Moonface was trying hard not to wince as Mr Watzisname dabbed at him.

'Don't trouble yourself, dear Watzisname, they're only trifles,' said Moonface.

'I don't know, old chap, you've cut yourself quite badly. Perhaps I should try to stitch you up. You don't want to be left with scars all over your distinctive face,' said Mr Watzisname, eyeing his sewing basket in the corner.

'Thank you, but *no* thank you!' Moonface said quickly. 'I shall wear my scars with pride. I rescued my Silky from an evil prince! A giant of a man, at least three metres tall, but I soon taught him a lesson!'

This was such an outrageous distortion of the facts that Milo's eyes popped, but he didn't say anything. His expression made it clear what he was thinking however, and Moonface added, 'But I daresay I came off worst. But I was willing to suffer any punishment to get Silky back!'

'That's true,' said Milo.

He was looking at Silky, who was still tearful. 'You see how much you mean to Moonface,' Milo said gently.

Silky nodded, wiping her eyes, though tears went on spilling down her face.

'Dear Moonface,' she murmured, but she still seemed very dazed and dreamy.

'Dear, dear Silky,' said Moonface. 'You look so tired and wan after your ordeal. I think you'd better go straight to bed and have a nice, long rest. I'll bring you a glass of cordial – and Toffee Shocks are very restorative.'

The children stared. This seemed a brand-new Moonface!

They were all actually very tired, so after they'd thanked the Saucepan Man and Mr Watzisname for their kind hospitality they started to make their journey down the Faraway Tree. Mia and Birdy helped tuck Silky up in bed. She had a long white nightdress – and as soon as she put it on, her wings faded to white too. Even her cheeks lost their colour.

'I'm sure you'll feel better soon,' Mia whispered, giving her a goodnight kiss.

'And Moonface is trying so hard to please you,' said Birdy. 'He's really much nicer than Prince Hunter, even if he's not quite as handsome.'

'Night, night, sleep tight,' said Pippin. 'I'll come and peep at you in a while to see if you need a cuddle.'

Silky did manage a small smile then. They left her curled up in her little bed and went to Moonface's house. It was looking pretty chaotic – and there were still no candidates for the role of cushion fetcher.

'I'll just take Silky her cordial and Toffee Shock, and then I'll start clearing up,' Moonface said resolutely.

'Maybe you should have a rest first,' said Milo. 'To give your battle scars time to heal.'

'You were very brave, Moonface,' said Mia.

'You knocked Prince Hunter's crown right off!'

said Birdy.

'Yes, I did, didn't I?' said Moonface, smiling widely, as he gave everyone a Toffee Shock.

Then the children slid down the slippery-slip. Pippin went with them, and then gathered up their cushions.

'Maybe I could be the cushion gatherer!' he said, jumping up and down. 'Do you think Moonface might pay me in Toffee Shocks?'

It seemed a splendid idea. Milo, Mia and Birdy paused for a few moments by the Faraway Tree's huge roots, still not quite sure of the way out of the Enchanted Wood. But then a blue tit flew out of its nest and hovered above them.

'Look, it's a little blue bird – and I'm little blue Birdy!' said Birdy, holding out her tattered princess skirts.

The blue tit twittered as if it was laughing and then flew a short way, and then flew back to them.

'It's telling us to follow!' said Birdy.

So they ran along beneath it and in a matter of minutes the trees thinned out and their *wisha-wisha-*

wisha became a whisper. The children jumped over the ditch and rushed back to the cottage.

It felt as if they'd been gone for days, but Mum and Dad were still sitting happily in the kitchen chatting over their coffee.

'Oh my goodness, look at the state of you, Birdy!' said Mum. 'Your poor princess outfit! Change into your shorts, sweetheart, and I'll pop it in the washing machine for you.'

'It's OK, Mum. I'm not sure I want to wear it ever again. I'm a bit tired of playing princesses,' said Birdy. 'In fact I'm a bit tired altogether at the moment!'

Mum and Dad seemed happy to have a quiet relaxing day at home, so the children managed a rest too. In the afternoon Mum decided to do a bit of baking. It was rather a surprise, because the only thing she'd ever tried to bake before was a loaf of sourdough bread and it hadn't been a success.

'I thought we could have special cakes for tea,' she said. '*Fairy* cakes.'

All three children helped with the mixing (and took turns scraping the bowl) and the fairy cakes turned out splendidly – though they were all one flavour and they didn't whirl round and round. Dad spent the afternoon working on his wood sculpture.

The children stared at it. It was shaped like a very tall tree now, with many leafy branches. There were two little figures on the branches. They were still very roughly hewn, but one had a lot of hair and the other a very large round head.

'Who are the people in the tree, Dad?' Milo asked.

'Search me!' said Dad. 'They just sort of shaped themselves. They do look a bit weird though. Shall I chop them off?'

'No!' said Mia. 'No, Dad – they seem as if they belong there.'

'Could you try to make this one look a bit prettier though?' said Birdy, pointing to the figure with the long hair. 'She looks like a fairy to me.

'Well, this other one certainly isn't fairy-like,' said Dad. 'I'm going to have to scrape some of that head away – it looks all wrong.'

'I think it looks just right,' Birdy insisted. 'I *like* its head. It's so round, just like the moon.'

The children discussed their parents as they went up to bed.

'What do you think made Mum make fairy cakes?' said Mia.

'And why's Dad carving that tree all of a sudden?' said Milo.

'They can't know about the Faraway Tree, can they?' said Birdy.

'I'm sure they don't,' said Mia. 'Not unless they go there when we're fast asleep, and they'd never leave us alone in the house.'

'Maybe a little magic from the Enchanted Wood is leaking out all the way into our cottage?' Birdy suggested. 'Sometimes when I'm going to sleep I think I can hear the trees going *wisha-wisha-wisha*.'

'I do hope Silky's all right now,' said Mia. 'Imagine her wanting to stay in the Land of Princes and Princesses.'

'Well, I wanted to stay too, just for a little bit longer,' said Birdy.

'I wonder what land it will be tomorrow,' said Milo. 'I hope it's somewhere really exciting.'

*

It was cool and windy the next day and Mum made them put jumpers on to play in the lane. Yet the moment they jumped over the ditch and set foot in the Enchanted Wood it suddenly seemed stiflingly hot, so much so that they had to pull their jumpers off immediately. They tied them round their waists so they wouldn't lose them. Birdy's kept coming undone, so Milo nobly tied her jumper round his waist too, though it was an itchy pink one knitted by their grandma, with little hearts and flowers as part of the pattern.

The trees went *wisha-wisha-wisha* very loudly, perhaps because their leafy branches were shaking in the strong wind. There was a strange smell in the air.

'What is it?' said Mia, wrinkling her nose. 'It smells a bit like bonfires, but dirtier than that.'

'Yes, like bad eggs,' said Milo. 'How weird!'

'I don't like it,' said Birdy. 'Shall we go back now?'

'It's probably just something rotting somewhere. We won't notice when we climb up high in the Faraway Tree,' said Milo.

'You want to see Silky and Moonface and Pippin, don't you?' said Mia.

Birdy nodded, but the smell grew stronger as they got nearer the Faraway Tree, and when they were standing right underneath it even Milo and Mia weren't sure they wanted to carry on.

'Let's just go as far as the Angry Pixie's house and ask if he knows what's causing the smell,' said Milo. 'I won't mind if he throws a jug of water at me today, because it's so flipping hot!'

The trunk of the tree was unpleasantly warm and there were scarlet pointy berries growing all over the branches. Mia loved all red berries and hoped they might be a new type of strawberry or raspberry. She bit into one – and then immediately spat it out, her eyes streaming.

'Yuck! It's like the hottest chilli ever! Don't try one, Birdy – it'll blow your head off!' she warned. She stuck her tongue out. 'I'm going to ask the Angry Pixie for a drink of water.'

But when they got to his house and tapped on his window he refused to open it, even though he'd made friends with the children now. They could see him standing there and he could certainly see them peering in at them, but he just shook his head and mouthed something they didn't understand.

'I think he's saying something about a land,' said Milo.

'The Land of . . . Agon?' said Mia. 'What's that?'

The Angry Pixie shuddered, pointed downwards and flapped his hands.

'He's telling us to climb down the tree and run away,' said Birdy. 'Shall we? I really, really don't like this horrid smell.'

'Perhaps we'd better go and see if Silky and Moonface and Pippin are all right first,' said Milo.

'Yes, this smell is going to be awful for Pippin. Animals have such sensitive noses,' said Mia.

'*I've* got a sensitive nose,' said Birdy, pulling her T-shirt up so that it covered her face.

'Well, I've got a sensitive throat, and it's burning like anything,' said Mia. 'But Silky will give me some lemonade, I'm sure.'

'I wish Dame Washalot would chuck some of her

soapy water down the tree to cool us off,' said Milo. 'I wouldn't mind being soaked to the skin today.'

They climbed up and up, the smell getting stronger and the bark getting so hot they wished they were wearing gloves. They came to Silky's door and knocked. And knocked again. And called her name.

'She's probably gone to visit Moonface and stick some new plasters on his poor face,' said Birdy. 'I do hope he's completely better now.'

They went to find out. Milo knocked on Moonface's door. They could hear a fearful muttering inside, many hushed voices, but the door stayed firmly shut.

'Moonface?' Mia called through his letter box. 'Are you in there? We've come to see if you're all right.'

The door opened a crack, and they saw Moonface's eye peering at them anxiously.

'Mia and Milo and Birdy! Oh, come in, my dears, come in right away – though I'm afraid it's very crowded!'

Moonface was not exaggerating. Silky and Pippin were in one armchair, the Saucepan Man and Mr Watzisname were in another, Dame Washalot was in the rocking chair and dozens of squirrels were crammed on the sofa, the red squirrel among them, trying to stop them wriggling. The littlest squirrels were all crying, wiping their eyes with their bushy tails.

Everyone looked anxious and distressed, especially Mr Watzisname, whose face was bandaged and his jacket and trousers seemingly covered in soot.

'What on earth has happened?' Milo cried.

Pippin rushed up to Mia and clutched her round the knees, whimpering.

Birdy started crying and ran to Silky.

'There now. It's going to be all right. We're quite safe here,' she said, though she didn't sound absolutely sure. Her dress was pearly grey and her wings were a darker grey and hung rather limply from her shoulders.

'We'll be fine as long as we all stay in here. If by any chance we hear an unwelcome visitor advancing, then we'll all slide down the slippery-slip. We don't think any of them could fit down it themselves,' said Moonface.

'*Them?*' said the three children.

'The Land of Dragons has come to the top of the Faraway Tree!' said Silky, shuddering.

CHAPTER TWELVE

'DRAGONS!' MILO gasped.

He had been passionate about dragons ever since
he was very small. He still took his dragon toy to
bed with him. He felt far too big to play with it now,
but it was comforting to stroke its velvet scales when
he couldn't sleep. He had watched dragon cartoons
and dragon TV series and dragon films, and he had
several dragon stories and a colouring book of all
different kinds of dragons. He'd even had a dragon
dressing-up costume with a fantastic snarling head,
and had very much enjoyed running around roaring
at his sisters.

Now there were real dragons right above his head! Milo should have known from the smell of sulphur and scorching that fiery creatures were nearby. Wonderful, extraordinary, powerful fire-breathing dragons!

'Dragons!' said Mia. She usually loved all creatures, real or mythological, but she had watched Milo's dragon films when she was very young, and they had given her nightmares. She'd had many terrible nightmares where they had invaded her bedroom and set it on fire and she'd woken up screaming. Mum or Dad had always come running to give her a cuddle and reassure her, but she'd always felt such a fool. She hated having to admit she was frightened.

'Dragons!' Birdy whispered. She was frightened of dragons too. She was frightened of lots of things: the shouty teacher at her school; the rather sweaty man in the shopping centre who pretended to be Father Christmas; the roaring sound and choking smell in busy swimming pools; very big cows; and going to the dentist. She had always comforted herself that at least dragons weren't real. Now they seemed all too real. She could smell them and feel their heat. A small, thin one might be poking his head through the cloud so that he could come slithering down the ladder any moment.

She looked at poor quivering Mr Watzisname with his bandage and burnt clothes.

'Did a dragon get you, Mr Watzisname?' she asked, trembling.

Mr Watzisname groaned. 'It's my own fault,' he mumbled. 'I should have realised. I woke very early and felt the heat and the strange smell and thought the Land of Bonfires had come. I love watching fireworks and eating sausages cooked on a bonfire, so I thought I'd pop up for an early breakfast while Saucepan was still sleeping.'

'If only I'd woken up too! I'd never have let you go up that ladder, dear chap,' said Saucepan.

'But I did – and the first thing I saw was a huge dragon rushing towards me! I managed to duck back down the ladder as it opened its mouth and missed the full horror of its flames, but I'm still pretty scorched!' Mr Watzisname moaned. 'I do hope I haven't lost my good looks!'

The children were rather surprised because Mr Watzisname was a particularly plain man, with a bulbous nose and a fair scattering of warts, but they expressed sympathy all the same.

'I promise you your burns are very light. You will be fully healed in a matter of days,' said Silky. 'And you will too, little squirrels. You must promise me not to go any further up the tree though, not until the Land of Dragons is gone.'

'*You* must promise *me* not to try to rescue any more people, Silky dear!' said Moonface. 'You're in even more danger than we are. You know the dragons are very keen on beautiful young girls – and you're the most beautiful ever!'

Moonface was clearly trying his hardest to make Silky feel protected and cherished now.

'Dragons like girls?' Birdy asked.

'They *eat* them,' said Mia, and then wished she hadn't, because Birdy looked so terrified.

'They wouldn't eat you, Birdy, I promise,' said

Silky. 'They're not going to hurt anybody, if we just stay here until their land whirls away. We've got plenty of food – Moonface has a huge tin of Toffee Shocks, and I've made some sandwich surprises to keep us going.'

Birdy wished she'd baked some cakes instead, but was actually delighted by the sandwiches. Silky had made tiny nut-bread cheese sandwiches on little sticks for the squirrels, which they licked like lollipops. When they bit into the cheese ball inside it went pop in their mouths and made them giggle. Dame Washalot had delicate cucumber sandwiches on a pretty patterned plate – and when she'd finished the sandwiches she started eating the plate itself because it was made of spun sugar so sweetly delicious it made her head spin round and round. The Saucepan Man and poor Mr Watzisname had big ham and pickle rolls, which set them chuckling at every mouthful, because it was special tickle pickle.

Moonface had a beef sandwich made with green spinach bread, and every time he took a bite the muscles popped in his arms and his round tummy flattened considerably. He ate his sandwiches admiring himself in his looking glass. Pippin had honey sandwiches of course, but perhaps they should have been called *hummy* sandwiches, because they hummed a tune as he nibbled them. He nodded his head and clapped his paws in time to the music, dripping quite a lot of honey in the process.

The children had ice-cream sandwiches – thick chocolate coating over creamy ice cream hiding little strawberry hearts – which tingled deliciously on the tongue. It was very soothing on Mia's sore throat. Silky let them eat another and then another.

Moonface went round pouring cherryade for everyone, with cowslip wine for Dame Washalot, Saucepan and Mr Watzisname, which cheered them tremendously. Mr Watzisname was given several glassfuls because of his terrifying ordeal. There was almost a party atmosphere in the round little room, though it grew hotter than ever and the smell of sulphur made them all feel faint.

Mr Watzisname nodded off to sleep with his

head on the Saucepan Man's shoulder and started snoring very loudly. Saucepan didn't mind too much because he was used to noise – in fact he was soon fast asleep too, snoring in harmony with his old friend. Moonface noticed how pale Silky was and insisted she lie down on his bed. He sat down at the end of it, watching over her like a guard dog until he fell asleep too.

Mia and Birdy and Pippin curled up together in a sticky huddle, their eyelids closing. Everyone was asleep now – except for Milo. He stayed wide awake and tingling with excitement. There were real live fire-breathing dragons right above his head! He couldn't miss this incredible opportunity. He could be the only boy in the whole world to see an actual true dragon! He'd never forgive himself if he didn't have just one peep. He needed only to poke his head above the cloud. He could duck down again if there were any dragons nearby.

He knew Mr Watzisname had been badly scorched, but he was an old gentleman and his reactions were very slow. Milo was sure he'd be able to dodge back to safety in time. He stood up and very stealthily started to make his way to the front door. One of the squirrels stirred and opened its eyes, but Milo put his finger to his mouth and the squirrel obediently kept quiet. Just as he reached the front door there was a sudden clink and clank as the Saucepan Man wriggled into a more comfortable position. Milo stood still, holding his breath. Saucepan started snoring again, so Milo dared turn the doorknob – and then he opened the door and was out!

The sulphur stung his nostrils and choked his throat, but he wasn't going to let anything stop him now. He shut the door carefully behind him and then started climbing up the tree. The trunk was so hot he could hardly bear to touch it, but he went at lightning speed, pressing his lips together determinedly.

He could barely see the ladder for smoke, and the cloud was a threatening deep grey, not its usual fluffy white. Milo was trembling now, but he clambered up. He imagined a dragon crouching beside the top of the ladder, its jaws open waiting to breathe fire at him, and it was such a terrifying thought that he very nearly gave up – but he had to take just one peep.

Then his head was through, and he found himself looking at a desolate dark land with blackened stumps of trees and scorched earth – but no dragon in sight. He pulled himself up and stepped on to the withered grass. It burnt his feet through his trainers, and his eyes stung so much he could barely see. He blinked hard and then suddenly saw two dragons to the right of him – two unmistakable scarlet dragons. One was large, its scales glistening in the eerie light, its head enormous, its spine sharply ridged, its tail whipping this way and that as it strode along on its powerful hind legs. The other was much smaller, not much bigger than Milo himself. Its eyes were big, its spine barely knobbed, its tail short and stubby. It gambolled along a little unsteadily. It was a baby dragon, newly hatched from its egg!

Milo gaped at the pair in awe. Here he was, standing in this barren land, staring at a mother and a baby dragon! He'd done it! If only Mum and Dad had let him have a mobile! Would anyone ever believe he'd seen dragons if he didn't have a photo to prove it? But he had seen them – the image would be there for ever inside his head and he would remember it until his dying day.

Then he was suddenly aware that the earth was vibrating underneath his feet, and the smell was even stronger. He turned his head – and there was a much larger dragon thundering towards him! It was blood red, its teeth clenched, smoke spurting out of its nostrils.

Milo ran for the ladder, screaming. He sprinted hard, not even drawing breath, knowing it was only a few strides and he was a good runner, the fastest in the whole school – but the great dragon reached out and gripped him by the back of the neck!

'Help!' Milo yelled. 'Help me! Help me!'

But there was no one to help. No one even knew he was there.

The dragon picked him up in its dreadful claws, swung him violently upside down and stared into

his eyes. Milo waited for the burst of fire. He was trying desperately to be brave. If he was going to die, then he wanted to do it courageously.

'I'm not afraid of you!' he said, which was probably the most ridiculous statement ever uttered.

The dragon opened its great mouth, showing jagged black teeth. Milo was almost overpowered by the great heat from its throat. He could see flames flickering round its tonsils – but it swallowed them down. It started shaking, making grunting noises. It seemed to be *laughing*.

'It's not funny!' Milo said furiously, kicking out at it. There was a smell of burning rubber from his trainers, and they turned black, scorching his feet. 'Go on then! Burn the rest of me! Just get it over with!'

The dragon laughed louder. It shook so much, Milo could feel it slightly loosening its grip. He kicked out again, and waved his arms around, wondering if he could possibly wriggle right out of the monster's grasp.

'Stop squirming, small girl!' said the dragon.

It spoke in a strange crackling voice, as if on a very bad telephone connection – but it was definitely speech.

'I didn't know dragons could speak!' said Milo, interested in this new fact in spite of his extremely perilous situation.

'I have encountered many tender young maidens since the Time of the Ancients, when we roamed the whole world, not just our own airborne land,' said the dragon. 'I am familiar with many human tongues. Mmm, tongues just happen to be the juiciest little titbits!' A drool of boiling saliva dribbled down its scaly chin.

Milo wondered if it would be better to be eaten alive or burnt to death. There didn't seem much in it. Perhaps burning would be quicker.

'You wouldn't want to eat me,' he said. 'I'm a boy, so I'm probably as tough as old boots.'

The dragon held him closer, inspecting him with its bloodshot eyes.

'Of course you are a maiden. You are wearing a pink gown and you have extremely abundant hair,' it

said, peering at Birdy's jumper flapping at his waist
and Milo's generous locks. 'You look extremely
tender – a perfect small maiden for my son's first
solid food.'

Milo turned his head as best he could upside
down and saw the very small dragon hopping up and
down excitedly, with the mother dragon rubbing her
claws together and thumping her tail.

'I think I'd make him sick,' Milo said quickly.
'You wouldn't want me to make him ill, would you?'

'Nonsense, maiden, you look like very prime
young flesh,' said the dragon. 'Now, wife, shall we
fry her gently first, or should we let our dear son
nibble her raw?'

'Perhaps we could breathe on her at the last
minute so that she's just slightly seared,' said the
mother dragon thoughtfully. 'I think this calls for a
celebration. We shall hold a party for our number
one son. The first flesh tasting is a very important
event!'

The big dragon carried Milo to a blackened tree
stump and tied him to it tightly by the wrists and

ankles with twine. Milo struggled, doing his best to wriggle out of his bonds. He had seen it done in many movies: one twist of the wrist, a shake of the ankle, and with one bound the hero was free. But this wasn't a film and Milo didn't feel much of a hero. The dragon twine stayed firmly in place.

The mother dragon scurried off to invite all their friends and neighbours to the celebration, while the big dragon sat back and gloated, spitting occasionally so that little gobbets of fire sizzled all round poor Milo. The baby dragon strutted about, rubbing its scaly stomach in anticipation.

Milo tried very hard to keep his chin up proudly and look noble and courageous, but he couldn't help his eyes watering. Perhaps it was because of the smoke and the sulphurous stench.

Meanwhile . . . Mia was the first to wake up in Moonface's round room. She rubbed her stinging eyes and coughed to clear her burning throat. She looked about her, checking Birdy and Pippin, who were cuddled up together. And Milo was . . . ? He wasn't squashed in the chair with the Saucepan Man and Mr Watzisname. He wasn't sharing the other armchair with Dame Washalot. He wasn't by the bed with Silky and Moonface. He wasn't on the sofa among all the little squirrels.

'WHERE'S MILO?' Mia shouted.

Everyone woke, rubbing their eyes and groaning. They looked round and up and down. Moonface even looked under his bed.

'He wouldn't have gone outside, would he?' he said anxiously.

Mia was biting her knuckles. She knew Milo was obsessed with dragons. But even so, surely he wouldn't have been reckless enough to go to have a look at them?

'I think he could have gone up the ladder!' she said.

'He wouldn't have done that!' said Silky. 'Milo's such a sensible boy. He knows just how dangerous it is.'

'And he's seen what happened to my poor old chum,' said Saucepan.

'Birdy, what do you think?' said Mia.

Birdy screwed up her face. 'I think he *might* have gone to see those horrid dragons,' she said.

'Then we must go after him and drag him back!' said Mia determinedly.

'You can't go anywhere near the ladder, let alone up into Dragon Land!' said Moonface. 'You're a maiden, Mia – and you are too, Birdy, though a very little one. The dragons would eat you up!'

'I'll be as quick as quick can be,' said Mia. 'Not you, Birdy – you know you fall over when you run hard. I'll go and get him.'

'You can't possibly outrun a dragon!' said Silky. 'I'll go. I don't need to run. I can seize Milo and fly away with him.'

'No, you're staying here, Silky – it's not safe for you, even though you have wings!' said Moonface. He was very pale and trembling, but utterly resolute. 'I shall go!'

'I shall go too!' said Saucepan. 'Not you, dear Watzisname – you're already battle-scarred. But Moonface and I will rescue young Milo. We will arm ourselves with my saucepans and fling them at the scaly monsters.'

'I shall come too! I am definitely not a young maiden!' said Dame Washalot, rolling up her sleeves. 'Look at my big, strong arms from doing all that washing and scrubbing over the years! I shall pummel those pesky dragons into submission!'

'And I'll bite their ankles!' said Pippin.

'And we'll climb up and bite their bottoms!' said Tipkin, and all the other squirrels cheered and brandished their bushy tails.

'You're all so wonderfully kind, but Milo's my brother, so I'm the one who should go after him,' said Mia.

'And he's my brother too, and I absolutely promise I won't fall over when we snatch him back from the horrid dragons,' said Birdy.

'My dear friends, you're all so touchingly brave and determined, but the dragons are huge evil creatures who can set fire to you at fifty paces,' said Moonface. 'I utterly insist that you all stay here in safety. I am the only one with any chance of conquering the dragons because I am Moonface the

Magician!' He puffed himself up proudly, though his teeth were chattering.

They stared at him. The red squirrel folded his arms.

'But your magic tricks have a habit of going wrong!' he pointed out unkindly. 'Look what happened to my poor son!'

'Oh, Daddy, don't be mean,' said Tipkin. 'I *liked* being teeny-tiny.'

Moonface suddenly gave a start. 'Aha!' he cried, pumping his fist in the air. Then he looked at Silky. 'Stay safe, my dearest love,' he whispered, and then ran from the room.

Silky clasped her hands. 'Oh, Moonface!' she cried. She couldn't stay. She ran after him. And Mia ran after Silky and Birdy ran after Mia and Pippin ran after Birdy and Dame Washalot ran after Pippin and Saucepan ran after Dame Washalot and poor scorched Mr Watzisname ran after Saucepan and all the squirrels swarmed round their feet. They all climbed the tree as fast as they could and clambered up the ladder, almost tumbling over each other in their haste. They poked their heads out of the cloud one after another – and all gasped.

There was Moonface hurtling forward on his little legs – and somehow no knight in shining armour had ever looked so valiant. He was running headlong towards a great ring of dragons, huge and scaly with great jaws, some with black smoke puffing out of their nostrils. They were gathered round a blackened tree stump, where poor Milo was tethered. A smaller dragon was jumping up and down, with a tablecloth tied round its neck, acting as a bib. The biggest dragon of all was in the act of untying Milo, but there was no way he could ever break through the circle of dragons.

> 'Hubble, bubble, scratch my stubble,
> Waggle my ears and make eyes blink,
> Lick my lips and shake my hips,
> Point my pinky and make them SHRINK
> – but only the dragons!'

Moonface yelled at the top of his voice, gesturing as

he ran, and then pointing with his little finger at the dragons.

They roared and raged and steadied themselves to flame him, but before they could draw breath they started shrinking rapidly – heads, bodies, scaly limbs and tails. In two ticks they'd turned into the tiniest nail-size newts, and the baby dragon was only a pinhead. They scurried about, scarcely visible, in the tiniest puff of smoke.

'Hurray for Moonface!' everyone shouted, jumping out on to the scorched grass and leaping in triumph.

Moonface had reached Milo by now and was swiftly untying him. Milo clasped Moonface round his neck and hugged him, and then Silky and Mia and Birdy and Pippin joined in the hug too, while Saucepan and Dame Washalot and Mr Watzisname danced a jig and all the squirrels did pawstands, waving their tails in the air.

'Shall we stamp on all the little whatsits?' said Mr Watzisname, wanting revenge.

It was a very tempting thought, but Mia argued

against the idea. Dragons might have been terrifying, menacing creatures who had been eager to eat her brother, but they were still animals. She couldn't quite love them, but she was willing to understand their nature.

'They can't really help it,' she said. 'They're like lions and tigers and crocodiles, programmed to think of us as food.'

'Oh, dear, this one's already dead,' said Milo, scooping up a tiny crushed dragon. It rested in the palm of his hand. 'I could take it back home! People will be amazed! The Natural History Museum might put it on display! The only dragon corpse in the world!'

'Or they might just think it's a very small species of newt,' Mia muttered to Birdy, but they were both so relieved that their brother was safe that they didn't tease Milo.

The Saucepan Man kept a box of matches in one of his kettles for when he fancied boiling up water for a cup of tea, so he emptied them out and gave Milo the box.

'Thank you, Saucepan,' said Milo gratefully. Then he turned to everyone. 'I was so silly and reckless to come up here, especially when you all warned me it was very dangerous. Thank you so, so much for being so brave and coming to rescue me. And especially thank *you*, Moonface, for being so quick thinking. You really are a hero!'

'Better than any prince!' said Silky, and she gave him a kiss on his great white cheek. 'Let us leave this barren land and go back to our dear tree right away. We'll have Celebration Pudding!'

Everyone cheered. Milo, Mia, Birdy and Pippin had no idea what Celebration Pudding was like, but it sounded splendid. They all hurried back down the ladder, Milo clutching his dragon in the matchbox as a souvenir of his adventure.

Saucepan and Mr Watzisname stayed on guard by the ladder, just in case a weeny dragon army snorting tiny fireballs invaded the Faraway Tree. They both held a saucepan at the ready. Silky sent Pippin up with two platefuls of Celebration

Pudding, and he also scampered down the tree with a bowl for the Angry Pixie, who had no idea that the rest of the Faraway Tree community had undergone such an astonishing adventure in the dreaded Land of Dragons.

The tree was already cooling, and the fiery scarlet berries were withering away. The choking smell of sulphur was dispersing on the breeze. Dame Washalot let Milo have a thorough bath in her washtub first, and then set about rewashing all the linen hanging on her washing line, cheerily singing as she scrubbed. She fortified herself every few minutes with a spoonful of Celebration Pudding and several sips of acorn wine.

The squirrels helped themselves secretly to acorn wine too and became very silly and giggly, until the red squirrel had to herd them up and tuck them all into bed to sleep it off. He rewarded himself with a double helping of Celebration Pudding.

Then Milo, Mia, Birdy, Pippin and Moonface sat cosily with Silky in her pretty house eating big bowlfuls of Celebration Pudding. It proved to be a

glorious mixture of everything delicious: a circle of meringue filled with a layer of ice cream and then mixed berries and sliced bananas in colourful rings with whipped cream, further decorated with tiny doughnuts bursting with jam and weeny eclairs filled with cream and little chunks of chocolate cake. Every bite was so delicious that it made everyone spontaneously sing *'Celebration!'*. Singing with your mouth full is not a pretty sight, but they were all so happy and relieved that manners didn't really matter.

The children had no idea what time it was of course, but they were so exhausted after the Land of Dragon adventures that they felt it was time they trailed back home. Pippin was already fast asleep, clutching his bowl, Celebration Pudding all round his mouth and smeared down his chest. Silky was lying on the sofa, taking it easy at last. Moonface was determinedly tackling the washing-up!

'Thank you so much again! See you tomorrow,' said Milo.

'And tomorrow!' said Mia.

'And tomorrow and tomorrow and tomorrow,' said Birdy.

They took a shortcut down Moonface's slippery-slip and left their cushions in a neat pile for Pippin to collect when he woke up. Then they walked hand in hand through the Enchanted Wood towards to the cottage, while the trees went *wisha-wisha-wisha*.

'Maybe it'll be the Land of Wish-Wish-Wish tomorrow!' said Birdy.

'Then I shall wish to meet up with my sea unicorn again!' said Mia.

'Well, I *don't* think I shall wish to see any more dragons,' said Milo. 'I'll just wish we can keep coming back to the Faraway Tree every single day till the end of the summer holidays.'

'Then *I'll* wish we can come back next summer. I want to go back to the Land of Princes and Princesses, so I can visit that palace again,' said Birdy.

'Well, I want to go to the Land of Bouncy Castles again – that was so much fun,' said Milo.

'I wonder what other magic lands there are?' said

Mia. 'We could ask Mum and Dad if we could come back at Christmas. Imagine the Enchanted Wood in the snow with the Faraway Tree hung with decorations and little presents!'

'We wish, we wish, we wish,' the three children sang, while the trees whispered above them.

AUTHOR'S NOTE

I absolutely loved Enid Blyton's Faraway Tree books when I was young. The Enchanted Wood was the first full-length book I read by myself. I started off pointing under the words on each line, muttering under my breath. By the time I was halfway through I was racing along, lost in this imaginary world, desperate to find out what was going to happen next.

I forgot that I was actually reading. I was climbing the Faraway Tree with the children in the story, meeting all the quirky folk who lived there, and scrambling up the ladder into the clouds at the top of the tree, discovering new magical lands. I adored Silky the fairy and wanted her to be my best friend. I loved Moonface and hoped he'd share his Toffee Shocks with me. I sang along with the Saucepan Man and tried to make up my own silly songs.

I read the other stories in the series until I almost knew the Faraway Tree books by heart. I couldn't decide which magic land was most exciting. It was probably the Land of Birthdays, but did I want my own pony, a doll that came alive or the ability to fly?

I started making up my own magic lands, writing down my stories in little notebooks. It seems so wonderful now, many years later, that I've been asked to write this brand new adventure in the Faraway Tree series. I do hope you've enjoyed reading about Milo, Mia and Birdy. Did you like meeting up with Silky and Moonface and Saucepan, and all their Faraway Tree friends? Would you choose to go with them to the Land of Unicorns, the Land of Bouncy Castles, the Land of Princes and Princesses or the Land of Dragons?

Perhaps we can all jump over the ditch into the Enchanted Wood another time!

photo © Jiksaw

JACQUELINE WILSON

Jacqueline Wilson has been writing since she was 9 years old. She is one of Britain's bestselling and most beloved children's authors. The creator of Tracy Beaker, Hetty Feather and many other memorable characters, she has written more than 100 books and won numerous prizes. *The Magic Faraway Tree* was her favourite childhood story.

MARK BEECH

Mark Beech was born in Pendle, Lancashire, and loved to draw from an early age. His very popular work regularly includes scary dragons, wild dinosaurs, grumpy witches and many other wacky creatures. Mark lives in the Forest of Bowland, where he enjoys walking with his dog Bungle.

Meet our
FARAWAY TREE FRIENDS

BIRDY is the youngest in the family and loves fairies, dressing up and her toy dog Gilbert.

MIA is the second eldest and is very fond of animals and drawing in her sketchbook. She hopes to be a vet one day.

MILO is the eldest sibling and loves running, playing video games and making things with wood.

MOONFACE lives at the very top. In his house is the start of the slippery-slip, a huge slide that curves all the way down inside the trunk of the tree.

SILKY lives below Moonface. She is the loveliest fairy you could ever imagine.

THE SAUCEPAN MAN is funny and he's great at making up songs. His saucepans make lots of noise when they jangle together.

Have you read

Enid Blyton's

original three books?

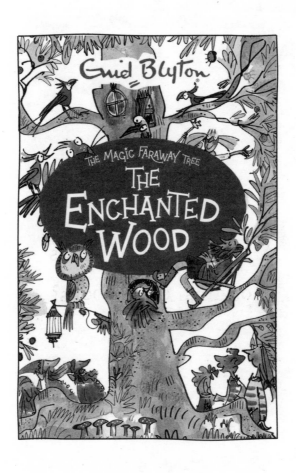

'Up the Faraway Tree,
Joe, Beth and me!'

Joe, Beth and Frannie move to the country and find
an Enchanted Wood right on their doorstop! And in
the wood stands the Magic Faraway Tree where the
Saucepan Man, Moonface and Silky the fairy live.
Together they visit the strange lands which lie at the
top of the tree. They have the most exciting
adventures – and plenty of narrow escapes!

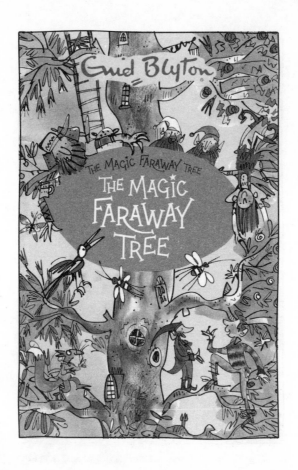

*'Oh, do let's take our lunch up into
the Land of Topsy-Turvy. Oh, do, do!'*

Rich thought it would be dull in the country with
Joe, Beth and Frannie. But that was before he found
the Magic Faraway Tree!
They only have to climb through the cloud at the
top of the huge, magical tree to be in the Land of
Spells, or the Land of Topsy-Turvy, or even the
Land of Do-As-You-Please!

Joe, Beth and Frannie are fed up when they hear
that Connie is coming to stay – she's so stuck-up
and bossy. But that won't stop them from having
exciting adventures with their friends Silky the
fairy, Moonface and the Saucepan Man.
Together they climb through the cloud at the top of
the tree and visit all sorts of strange places, like the
Land of Secrets and the Land of Treats – and
Connie learns to behave herself!

Also available

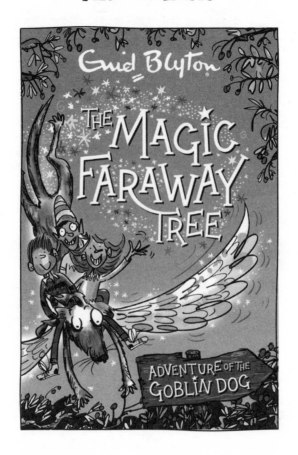

a stand-alone Magic Faraway Tree adventure
by Enid Blyton.

Travel to the top of the Magic Faraway Tree with
Peter and Mary and explore Fairyland, where you'll
encounter the Goblin Dog, rescue a princess and
visit the Land of Storytellers.

Enid Blyton

is one of the most popular children's authors of all time. Her books have sold over 500 million copies and have been translated into other languages more often than any other children's author.

Enid Blyton adored writing for children. She wrote over 700 books and about 2,000 short stories. *The Famous Five* books, now 80 years old, are her most popular. She is also the author of other favourites including *The Secret Seven*, *The Magic Faraway Tree* and *Malory Towers*.

Born in London in 1897, Enid lived much of her life in Buckinghamshire and loved dogs, gardening and the countryside. She was very knowledgeable about trees, flowers, birds and animals. Dorset – where some of the Famous Five's adventures are set – was a favourite place of hers too.

Enid Blyton's stories are read and loved by millions of children (and grown-ups) all over the world. Visit enidblyton.co.uk to discover more.

Illustration by
Laura Ellen Anderson.